Blighted Blues

Published by
Adonis & Abbey Publishers Ltd
P.O. Box 43418
London
SE11 4XZ
http://www.adonis-abbey.com

First Edition, April 2005

Copyright © M. O. Ené

British Library Cataloguing-in-Publication Data
A catalogue record for this book is available from the
British Library

ISBN 0-9545037-1-6

Cover Design   Ifeanyi Adibe

Printed and bound in Great Britain by Lightning Source
UK Ltd.

Blighted Blues

By M. O. Ené

Adonis & Abbey
Publishers Ltd

PREFACE
The chants of ants

Chrys sat on a craggy cushioned chair with his left forearm wedged between his chin and thigh, as if physically preventing his mouth from uttering a word. The Education & Welfare Committee meeting dragged on. After the tattering reports of society reps, the next item on the agenda was the welfare of overseas students. Usually, Chrys would be asked to report. Daphne, the very vocal women affairs officer, decided she knew better. She was chairing the meeting in place of the Union president. For five long and boring minutes, she preached that the problem confronting overseas students was covert racism.

"Excuse me, Daph, you are towing the old line of defence for the inadequacies of this Union's policies towards a section of student population."

"I do not think that is the true nature of things," Daphne declared matter-of-factly, looking around for supportive nods. No one spoke as she kept gnawing her chewing gum at sharp strokes like a nanny goat in labour.

Chrys continued, "There are little things the Union can do to improve life on campus for everyone, but we are always searching for specks in other people's eyes. We forget the logs in our own eyes." He referred to his circulated memo. Not one member had read it. They began to skim through it. He let them.

4

To pilot the meeting out of its self-imposed silence, Daphne said, "We can use the proposed Awareness Week to highlight all forms of discrimination. The Union...."

Chrys interjected, "I can give you a long list you can fit into Awareness Week: sexism, anti-Semitism, ethnocentrism, jingoism, bigotry, xenophobia, homophobia, gerontophobia... all forms of discrimination you can sing about. Let's look at the concrete issues outlined in my memo."

Not wanting to get into a shouting match, Daphne stated, "Okay, Chrys. Now, the London Demo: what is the latest from National Union?"

Chrys turned visibly livid. "Typical! We spend over an hour talking about lesbians and gays and we brush aside pressing problems that affect overseas students. Who cares with whom one chooses to sleep? Do not tell me celibacy is an archaic Vatican value." Everyone was taken aback. It was unlike Chrys to explode like that. He continued, "A demonstration against government-guaranteed top-up loans? You should be lucky you have a source for loans! Has the Union ever raised a finger as the overseas-student fees increase annually at a rate far above that of inflation? This must be the only place we microwave the few geese that lay golden eggs. This is what I call designer discrimination."

Chrys paused and then said, "Excuse me, guys; I think I have better things to do with my time." As he made for the door, he distributed the proposal he had written on how to curb alleged sexism in exams, an issue raised during the previous meeting.

****

Chrys Chiké Chimé was not keen in student union activities; the welfare of overseas students was his portfolio. He was eager to leave a mark. The first thing that struck him was the lack of a forum for foreign students to meet and discuss common problems. The Union supported ethnic clubs, euphemistically tagged "social clubs." The divide-and-rule policy, he reckoned, created a ghetto-like attraction that easily sucked in and separated new students from the mainstream. Thus, integration into the socio-academic environment eluded them. Without any reasonable interaction outside the classrooms, the ignorance and prejudice of home students deepened.

****

Back at his bed-sit accommodation on Welbeck Avenue, a two-minute drive down and off University Road, Chrys dropped his file jacket on the kitchen table and put on the kettle. The phone rang as he took a sip of the copiously creamed coffee.

"Hello?"

"Chiké, it's me, Adaora. I've been trying to reach you."

"I was attending a meeting. What's up?"

"You remember what you said about frogs, sorry, toads not doing midday jumps for fun?"

"Uh-huh," Chrys responded.

"Well, will it be all right if I come down tomorrow?"

"Praise the Lord!" he exclaimed. "Of course, it's all right."

His conversation with Adaora over, Chrys called his girlfriend Jackie, who lived in nearby Granby Grove with four other girls. One of the girls, an exchange student with a disembodied German accent, informed him that Jackie had gone to see a Union film.

****

Chrys came back late from clubbing and crashed onto his bed. The bed was only beginning to settle down from an imaginary intergalactic spin when the phone rang.

"Out drinking again, have we?" Jackie's voice dripped with unmasked sarcasm.

"Huh? Blimey! What time is it now, love?"

"Eleven thirty."

"Holy Milingo! Darling, I'm cancelling the Isle of Wight trip. My cousin is coming down from London. Say, why don't we drive down to Burseldon and shop at Tesco supermarket?"

"Listen, lover boy: Last week I returned the Blockbuster new-release unwatched. You were too tired… conference stress, you said. You worked all week. Yesterday, you would not come to a free film. Some stupid meeting...."

"Education & Welfare…."

"Who cares? You stay out all night boozing with shebeen trollops... and in that den of drug dealers, drug-crazed pimps, and prostitutes."

"Wow, wow! Hold your horses, darling. I went down to Sunshine Club in St Mary's with friends for a couple of pints; that's all."

"Excuse me? That's a den of hookers and social rejects."

Chrys dropped the handset on his bed. Jackie was not in any mood to hold a budgie; she would strangle the poor bird. The mere mention of St Mary's area shot up her adrenaline. And understandably too.

****

Months after Jackie had first arrived in Southampton, she went to the downtown area to buy some condiments from the international food shops. It was an early December evening, but it was already dark when she exited a food shop. A flashy, black BMW with white upholstery stopped beside her as she made her way to the bus stop. She assumed the decently clad driver needed directions. He turned out to be a kerb

7

crawler hoping to pick up an exotic hooker. St Mary's housed the city's red-light area, including the notorious Derby Road.

Jackie found the experience distressing because she had had a sheltered upbringing. However, she would not go to the University Counselling Unit. In her culture and at such trying times, people did not confide in total strangers. She met Chrys the following week at the Montefiore House launderette. Being of the same ethnic extraction as he and having a common cousin, she opened up. He listened. One thing led to another, and the listener became the lover. For months thereafter, Chrys treated Jackie like an eagle's egg.

****

This day, the supposedly precious egg looked as though it had hatched a vicious viper. Chrys picked up the phone and listened. Jackie was still talking. "And the trip we planned over a month ago, the trip we cancelled because you were writing a ten-page paper, is cancelled again. Your cousin is coming to town, so you went to celebrate in that downtown den of iniquities?"

"Damn it, Jackie, it was an academic paper, not some crass... I mean class essay! How am I supposed to know that she...?"

Jackie was hardly listening. She nagged on, "If I didn't know our cultural ethics on sexuality, I would say you are a closet gay."

"Bisexual, you mean?" Chrys wisecracked to get her attention.

"Right now, I can't vouch for you!" That was below the belt, but Jackie had not quite managed to grasp his sense of humour.

"Screw you, woman!" he blurted.

"I double-dare you!" She dropped the phone with a bang so hard his auditory hammers were stirred.

"Women!" Chrys gasped and thought to himself, "How can anyone refer to a conference paper presented at the impressive Palais de la Musique et des Congrès, Strasbourg, France on the effect of bureaucracy on the economic development of developing nations as merely 'a ten-page paper'?"

****

Adaora called after midday. She wanted to know how to get to Southampton, besides jumping onto the train at Waterloo and calling Chrys from Parkway or Central to pick her up. She was driving, and she was useless with maps. He advised her to take A316 and then M3 from Richmond. Once on M3, she would be in Southampton in an hour.

Chrys went to shop at the nearby Safeway Superstore. He called Jackie as soon as he came back, but she had gone to London for the weekend, or so another flatmate said.

He was far gone into cooking lunch when Adaora arrived. He was surprised that she came alone.

"I left the kids with a friend," she explained when they entered his room. "What are these newspaper cuttings all about?"

"They are for a casebook I was compiling on dictators."

"Bokassa. Banda. Bongo. Papa Doc Duvalier. Togo's Eyadema. Our Gowon… he is in good company! Mobutu Sese Seko. Mengistu, Obasanjo, and Said Barre? Idi Amin Dada. Wow, the Lion of Judea! Are you in a rush to die?"

"No, I want to open a comprehensive and critical casebook."

"I mean that after Rushdie, no publishers will touch it with a long pole."

"This is socio-political scene, published facts between hard covers. Besides, my subjects are hated, in hiding, beleaguered, or buried. They are in no position to sue. This is not religion, which is about fat faith and flaccid facts. I'm only collating facts, not fiction, and pointing out similar traits of megalomania and the consequences for fleeced folks. Do you know that in almost all the cases the Whitehall or the White House crops up?"

"Sure," Adaora answered. "I have this girlfriend Mary—I left my girls with her—whose sister wanted to do a doctoral study on the subject. A year later, her supervisor said it is all in her head, that it is… wait until you hear this mouthful: 'stereotypical anglosaxonophobic nonsense.' She abandoned the work."

Chrys took Adaora on the Isle of Wight cruise. It was dark when they came back to Southampton. She agreed to stay the night because they had not talked.

Adaora called London. "Hiya. Having fun? Listen, I can't make it back tonight…. You don't mind? Bless you, my dear! Yes, the *hunk* is besides me. 'Belly-button brother'? What is that? Get outta here! Mary, if you want to satisfy your morbid curiosity, say that when I come back. Of course I am sure he's my cousin…. Second. You wha'? Cousin in Christ? Listen, I have to hang up now. Thanks. Bye. Bye-bye!"

When they started talking, it took them into the holy hours of the morning. Adaora told Chrys all about her row with "the man they call my husband," and of her decision to move back to Nigeria. Her first move would be to divorce him.

Chrys counselled against such a step, especially with two young children. "It is not greener on this side. If you keep your ears to the ground, you will hear the chants of ants. The blacksmith that does not know how to forge a gong should look at the tail of a kite."

"I've had enough," she pleaded. "I have heard it said that the sheep that gave birth to a ram does not have a kid. I am married, but I am single. Like a bat, I am neither an aerial creature nor a land animal."

"Certain things in life sort themselves out with time. Unless you are leaving to clear your head, I suggest you stay here in England. Visit this Christmas and see for yourself. Whatever you do, Adaora, please do not just pack up and go."

The next morning, they worshipped at the Church of Immaculate Conception, just down the road in Portswood. After lunch, they strolled over to Jackie's. She had not come back from London.

"Have you spoken to the Italians lately?" Adaora asked, referring to Chrys's ex-wife and daughter in Perugia, Italy.

"A phone call now and then. I really miss her... my daughter Kamemena, I mean. My ex is bad news. I really should have stayed with the intemperate Italian to be in my daughter's life. No one should lose a chewy-sweet palm nut in an exhausted fireplace."

"I bet Jackie is better."

"Aren't they all the same?"

"Excuse me!"

"I'm sorry. Look at the time; I think you better make a move."

"I know. What a shame; I would have loved to stay some more."

"Please don't; you may have already cost me a girlfriend!"

Vintage Chrys's wisecrack turned out to be true. Someone saw him and Adaora on the Red Funnel ferry from the Isle of Wight to the Southampton Piers and told Jackie.

Hell hath no fury like Jackie supposedly scorned. In fact, hell had no more fury—she took it all.

1

If Jackie had burnt Chrys's car, he wouldn't have minded. The trouble with Jacqueline Ebere Onaga was that she would go on and on, until she was convinced she had wreaked enough havoc. It usually turned out to be overkill.

Jackie avoided Chrys for weeks. All efforts he made to see her proved fruitless. In a relatively small campus, avoiding him took some deliberate planning.

Unable to take it any longer, Chrys went over to her department and asked the secretary to get her. He claimed to be Jackie's brother; he had just flown in from Lagos, and he had a message from their father. It was easy for her to fall for his lie because in Nigeria every townsman outside the locality is a *brother*. She was visibly disappointed on seeing grinning Chrys, who went on to extract a cheap sister-brother hug. He egged her out of the secretary's office.

She agreed to talk.

They met that evening at Wessex Bar. Chrys tried very hard to make it up to her, but Jackie had made up her mind. He pressed on, "My dear, we should not rock the boat just because I was not around you for some time."

"What is the point in having a boyfriend if you can't have him, eh? No, I am going to make a clean break now that the term is still young. If we continue like this into my finals next session, I will either fail or, worse, have a heart attack."

"You are making a mountain out of mush," Chrys observed.

"Oh yeah? How come you didn't say your cousin is a she?"

"I tried to tell you it was Adaora, but you wouldn't listen."

"You never told me!" Jackie protested vigorously.

"'Shop at Tesco for a change,' remember? Why did I ask you to come and help me cook something decent?" Chrys paused as she picked up her gin and tonic with plenty of ice. "Please, Jackie, let us give it one more chance, huh? I will chuck the Union; we shall spend all weekends together, and there will be no more national meetings."

He went the extra mile and promised to cut off all extracurricular activities that would not involve her, including membership of E & W Committee. He also put on the block the office of Overseas Students Coordinator, which he had held for more than a year.

What Chrys considered his last try started off well in mid November. He wined and dined Jackie at Le Restaurant, which was down by the Docks. He couldn't believe his luck when she retired with him for the night. The rest was more than icing on his labour of love. She appeared to be responding to his pleas.

The next day, a rotten end-of-autumn Sunday, Jackie declared the agreeable affair dead. She said she was falling in love, and she did not want to get hurt. He thought she would come around to her senses sooner than later, but Jackie had stitched up her end of the tunnel.

That Chrys made it to the end of each long day was sheer miracle. As the cold clouds of December descended on the Solent, he began to accept the status quo. Jackie shunned his birthday party, which took place on the second Saturday. That was the final straw, probably her way of making the split official. Giving him the boot was bad, but he still wanted them to be friends.

13

Christmas hype was soon switched on; Santa's spend-spend XMAS season had come again. Chrys cancelled all social engagements. They made little sense without Jackie. He was going to sit back and lick his love wounds instead of fouling other people's Yuletide mood. Suddenly, the campus was deserted. Highfield, the off-city-centre area that housed the University, recaptured its suburban ambience. There were more pussycats about than humans. Loneliness or lonesomeness, whichever was worse, crept in. There was no denying the fact: he still loved her.

A full-grown adult after three decades, Chrys understood why the birth of a child two millennia before still thrilled believers and infidels alike. Immaculate Conception and the miracle of birth aside, nobody wants to be alone. Joseph and Mary travelling to Bethlehem demonstrated the power of family. In the usual mad rush to earn and spend, give and get, the prospect of a lonely Christmas abroad dawned on him. He had planned to spend the entire 90/91 holidays holed up with Jackie. Without the one-on-one *je ne sais quoi,* sharing with others seemed meaningless. Now the prospect of home alone stared him in the face.

Chrys decided to travel. There was no vacant seat in any scheduled flight to Lagos. The manager at Student Travel Agency (STA) promised to look out for any opening. Iraqi President Saddam Hussein had hinted that he might let go of his grudging "guests" for Christmas, so British Airways might decide to restore flights it had cancelled in readiness for an emergency airlift of Britons being used as human shield.

As he drove down the University Road, he decided to visit a compatriot in Montefiore. He turned left into Upper Shaftesbury and then right into Sirdar Road. After the Swaythling flyover, he saw Jackie. He pulled up beside her and opened the passenger's door.

"Hello, stranger! Hop in."

She entered. "Hi," she responded and closed the door.

"Do you want to send something to homefolk?" he asked as they approached the off-campus hostel complex.

"You're travelling to Enugu?"

"That's correct," Chrys confirmed.

Jackie thought about it for a minute and said, "Okay, I'll call you later in the week. I'll get off here, if you don't mind." She was going to A Block.

"At your service!" Chrys stopped in front of Stoneham House.

Opening the door to get off, she paused and tried to say something. Chrys listened. "Never mind," she said and alighted.

"Thanks for the beautiful birthday card and the precious present," he teased.

Jackie stopped and then walked on without responding to the tease. She had sent nothing to him. He knew.

For one week, Chrys buried himself in the library, reading back editions of political science and public administration journals. Evenings, he worked on his proposed casebook on dictators. He had sent synopses and sample chapters to publishers. Many sent back generic acknowledgement cards. Some sent straightforward thumbs-down: "We sadly regret... not suitable for our list." It didn't matter any more. He was venting. He didn't think serious publishers would invest in an unknown dreamer. Since he could not now afford subsidiary publishing, there was no harm in trying. After all, as they said in his hometown, "It is by dragging the he-goat around the marketplace that it eventually gets sold."

The book provided a pounding canvas. To increase his subject pool, Chrys roped in one-party political lords and zero-party practitioners. He was shifting the initial focus of his book, but here was an angry man looking for a vent, any vent, a butt to kick, any butt to shine his shoes.

2

Chrys was leaving for Christmas. STA secured a seat and phoned him immediately. He paid cash and collected the ticket within the hour. His mind was preoccupied with thoughts of end-of-year festivities in Nigeria, away from the rejection Jackie had dished out without mercy; ironically, her middle name, Ebere, means "mercy" in their native Igbo. She was yet to call as promised. He drove to the City Centre and picked up engraved jewellery from Samuels for his mother and gifts from Woolworths for his nephews and nieces.

Ready to leave, Chrys called Jackie again and left a final message: He was gone.

The taxi arrived sooner than expected, though it took more than the promised five minutes. He was at the door before the "God-Save-the-Queen" doorbell chime completed its course.

"Hi mate, you called for a cab?" a blob of a man inquired. His face was puffy and pleaded for a shave. His neck was completely tattooed. His wrist revealed that the pattern ran through his body. He was a mobile soft-porn gallery. "Going on 'oliday, are we?" He picked up the box and proceeded to the car parked just outside the dwarf metal gate.

"Hi, Ivy," Chrys called out to his landlady.

She was aware of his itinerary. She approached the door with Kylie. Chrys didn't like pets, but he liked Kylie—as long as the cat did not come into the room while he slept.

"Give my regards to all the members of your family."

"Thank you. I left my cousin's number in London and our home number, in case anybody desperately wants to get in touch. The country code is 234; the city code is 42."

The box locked away, Chrys sat in the back of the brown Vauxhall Cavalier. "No smoking" signs were displayed, but the car reeked of warm tobacco stench. The driver started the car, revved, and pushed the automatic gear into the <D> slot.

"Where to, mate?" the taxi driver requested.

"Lagos," Chrys responded absentmindedly.

"I don't think we can manage that on this banger, luv! Forget about Channel crossing and them Frogs, the flaming Sahara is something else. If Mark Thatcher couldn't make it, I've got no frigging chance."

"Oh, I am sorry; I thought the office told you. Parkway, please."

"That's more like it, mate," the driver chuckled, visibly impressed by his earlier remarks, which Chrys found bland coming from him.

The road to the Southampton Parkway Station had its fair share of traffic lights. The City Council appeared to prefer the lights to more expensive junction designs. In America, somebody would have calculated the penny-wise-pound-foolishness of such designs in terms of fuel economy, vehicular durability and drivability, safety, and human comfort. It could be held up in a court of law as the cause of increased stress-related debility. Trust the Yanks.

"Three pound twenty pee, luv," the driver announced as the squealing brakes brought the car to a stop behind another taxi in the rank.

Chrys gave him a fiver and asked for a pound back. The cabbie earned the 80 pence. He went through two yellow-to-red lights, and he helped with the box.

"Thank you," Chrys said and took his box.

"You 'ave a nice time, mate," the driver said as he put back his small bag of coins. "Me and the wife was in Egypt last year... sailed along them Nile, seen them Crocs and all."

"Interesting," Chrys said and silently thanked God for quiet taxi drivers.

The train was a slower service originating from further west in Weymouth, calling at most stations between Winchester, the administrative headquarters of Hampshire County, and Clapham Junction, the Queendom's busiest railway junction.

At London Waterloo, Chrys gathered his stuff and disembarked. He got a trolley, placed his box in it, and moved along with the one-way stream of commuters. Abandoning the trolley, he descended into the bowel of London earth. The Northern Line was not crowded. He disembarked at Embankment. He went on to the eastbound District Line and waited for a Barking train. A Circle Line train was leaving. The electronic sign showed his train would be coming in three minutes. It did.

When West Ham appeared, Chrys psyched himself to get off at the next stop: Plaistow. It would bring back all that had been bothering him, the pain he had decided to numb with the book. He was running away, yet everything he did seemed to remind him of her. He and Jackie had spent quality time in Plaistow, the residence of their common cousin Ossie.

Chrys dialled Ossie's number from a public phone. Vanessa was standing by. "I'll be there in four minutes flat," she said in her West Indian accent moderated by years in London and marriage to a Nigerian.

3

The road was relatively free. She had no problem negotiating the complex artery of roads. Vanessa had lived in London for most of her adult life. Her parents were originally from St Lucia, one of the smaller islands in the Caribbean, but she was born in Birmingham. She moved to London to stay with an aunt when her father left and her mother was not coping with two younger sisters and a dysfunctional brother. She stayed back in London to pursue a nursing career.

Vanessa coughed and looked at Chrys. "What is going on between you and Jackie?"

"Search me." Chrys knew that any hope of reconciliation would be snuffed out if Jackie knew he had talked about their rift with Vanessa.

"You know she is in the house." Vanessa revealed, as if trading the information for another from Chrys.

"I had a pretty good idea that you didn't bring your work home. Is she okay?"

"Yes, she is fine. She disappeared into the children's room after you phoned. I had to take food to her. What's going on?"

"What do you reckon, 'Nessa?"

"Ossie thinks it's normal with her."

"Time of the month, I suppose," Chrys joked.

Victoria Station. Chrys opened the door and collected his box from the backseat. He waved as she honked and drove off. He pushed his box on its inbuilt wheels for the few yards before picking up a trolley.

As he approached the British Airways offices, a lady standing by the door arrested his eyes. She was so stunningly beautiful Chrys could count how many men who did not turn round to take a second glance.

In her mid-to-late twenties, she wore a stylish skirt suit that fitted her as though it was designed on her, not just for her. Her hair was neatly done in a way that made her facial features stand out. Her gold-rimmed glasses blended with her permanently tanned, golden complexion. She was carrying a small travelling bag of the same colour as her knee-length coat. The fashionable coat had all the classic trench features with large, circular, bright-gold buttons. It was open, revealing her designer suit.

The lady looked as though she had just stepped off a spacecraft from Planet Prestige, as if she was conjured out of Vogue magazine and her bosom and backside retouched with a bit of firm but fresh flesh. She was a sight to behold. He stopped within a hearing distance to feed his eyes.

She was looking out as if she was expecting somebody. A slim-built youth of about 20, a bag of bones held together by a film of flesh, soon came rushing towards her with a big bag. The chap had a mop of strawberry blonde hair and wore tattered and dirty blue jeans. His sporty sweatshirt with drawstring hood had a bold-print inscription on the back: DILUTION IS NO SOLUTION TO POLLUTION.

"I can't stop," the chap said, "there's no parking for miles. You have a nice time and give my regards to Loretta."

"Oh Sean, I'm going to miss you," the lady said as she hugged him. She was older, much more mature, and extremely exotic. He kissed her on both cheeks and then lightly on the lips. He ran off and never looked back.

She bent down to pick up the bag. She couldn't quite manage it with the travelling bag, so she gave up and looked around. Their eyes met. Chrys recollected himself, released the trolley's brake bar, and wheeled his luggage towards the entrance.

"Hi. Do you mind if I share the trolley, please?"

"The pleasure would be mine," Chrys responded promptly. The bag was quite heavy; he repositioned himself and lifted it into the trolley. She noticed his discomfiture and smiled.

"Smashing," she said and glided gracefully away without looking back. She looked even better from behind. Her legs were firm and straight and appeared to have grown out of her daring derrière in a natural process of evolution.

He released the brake bar and moved on. Past the door, she was gone. Now, Chrys was worried. What if the bag contained Semtex explosive? The Scotland Yard Anti-Terrorist Squad had warned of renewed IRA campaigns in mainland Britain and had appealed for public vigilance. The Gulf crisis had added another dimension. Fear was rife that Saddam Hussein's men were on the move.

"I thought you had disappeared," the mystery mademoiselle said as he pulled up to the check-in counter for Lagos-bound passengers.

"It did cross my mind, sincerely speaking."

She smiled back, her lips stretching without opening. He looked at her more closely as she removed her lightly tinted glasses. The first thing that struck Chrys was the greenery of her eyes. No, one was green; the other was bright ripe-olive brown. He had never seen such eyes on anyone, or maybe she mismatched her differently coloured contact lenses.

"Are you going to Lagos?"

"Ain't that obvious?" she remarked. The other line was for Accra, Ghana.

"Well, I just wanna be sure. Are you?" Chrys wasn't going to be intimidated. He threw in some slang Americana for counter-effect.

"Yes."

It worked. He did not know what else to say. She had a steady stare that Chrys could not match. He tried twice to browbeat her, but she always came out tops. It must be the green eye. While he tried to figure out her eyes, she had them probing him. It was embarrassing.

He looked at the luggage quizzically as if weighing it optically. It had a leather nametag on which was written "FATIMA."

"May I call you Fati?"

"You certainly may not call me Fatty!" That sounded more like a warning than an objection to Chrys's choice of a shortened version of her supposed name.

He was not going to let the little communication conundrum mar the mental scenario of cuddling up with her in an air-conditioned room thousands of miles away from the indescribable English winter weather of 1990. It might not be, but daydreaming could be lots of fun.

Chrys toyed with the idea of a tactical withdrawal, but he would rather stoop low to conquer than stand and fight and lose. He apologized. She accepted. "Say then, fellow traveller, could you please look after *our* luggage while I get us the train tickets?"

"Sure," she said. She didn't seem to mind his choice of pronouns. Slowly, a serene smile swept across her face starting from the jade eye and culminating in a surprisingly deep dimple that began to disappear as the lower lips gradually parted to reveal what looked like divine dentures put in place by the good Lord on the morning of creation. It was not just the densely packed and Omo-white set of teeth—thirty-two strong and

23

correctly positioned—that arrested his attention, their evenness and shine and the natural hairline split in the upper row had a hypnotic, Close-up appeal.

"Good God," Chrys mumbled to himself. "Lazarus could not have felt more pleased when his sisters got Jesus to endorse an exceptional extension of his visa to planet Earth."

The train-ticket queue was not long, but it was not express service either. He assumed the lady was not a compatriot because her English had no detectable African accent. It was almost BBC-English, somewhere between astute assertiveness and bedroom-sexy velvet voice. However, it had a touch of northern accent—a slight Scottish or inherent Irish inflection. She must have picked that up from friends, just like her unnecessary American slang. Talking of friends, Sean is Celt.

Chrys had to make a lot of deductions by gradual elimination. It was not a tall order getting to know a compatriot. The best indicator was the unofficial Nigerian lingua franca, Naijâ—an evolved English slang rich in lexical items from local languages of Niger area.

"Hi, it took you quite some time? Did you get the tickets?" she asked.

"Sure, that one no be *wahala*," Chrys said, answering the last question first. She smiled. She understood. "I know say the line no *dey* move that fast."

"No be too *sabi* dey kill *una*," she responded.

That did it. Nobody ever learnt to so philosophise in Naijâ without living it. She even used *"una"* in place of plural "you," and *"sabi"* in place of "know," which meant she was in the know.

Chrys gave her the nosegay he had bought off a gypsy woman. It brought out a more beautiful and different being.

It got to their turn. She stepped aside. He placed the two boxes on the scale. They clocked 77.5 kilograms. The clerk took their tickets. "Did you pack the luggage yourself?"

"Yes," she responded.

"And nobody had access to the contents since you locked it?"

"That is correct," Chrys answered, forgetting all about the thought of possible explosive in her luggage. Nothing could be more appealing at that point than to be blown to Venus in her arms.

"Would you prefer the window or the aisle?"

"Neither would make any difference 33,000 feet up there," Chrys joked and looked at his publicly acknowledged companion.

They all laughed. Chrys waited to collect their tickets and, on the pretext of sorting out which was which, he would find out her last name because many Nigerian surnames tell a thousand and one stories. Either by design or instinctively, she reached out and took her ticket, which was in a colourful BA envelope; his was in the original STA cover.

4

The ten-fifteen train left on schedule. The driver pledged a 30-minute, non-stop ride and thanked passengers for choosing the British Rails, as if they were spoilt for choices.

A steward with a fake ponytail and a salesman voice wheeled in a trolley of several steaming stuff. "Coffee? Tea?"

"Coffee please," Chrys's companion requested. "Black, no sugar."

Chrys gave him a pound coin; 25 pence was tip.

The Gatwick Express arrived at the North Terminal via the Transit connection. It arrived later than scheduled. It had stopped for unknown reasons at Gloucester Road Junction and at Redhill.

They walked to the Flight Departure Hall. There were vacant seats near the check-in counters. As she dropped her travelling bag, it burst open in protest. Chrys was very close to her, and he smelt a whiff of alcohol. The sweet smell of her Poison perfume could not mask it.

"Leave it; let me have a look." She obliged. Chrys was not interested in the contents, but he could not help taking note of certain items. "Do look after my briefcase and the bag; these guys seem to be serious about destroying unattended luggage."

He went over to the bookshops and bought some weeklies and an *Officier Swisse* jack-knife. Twenty yards away from where he had left his companion minutes earlier, Chrys saw above all the heads of intending passengers and other motley crowd, a towering, middle-

26

aged man with a flowing, traditional *agbada* attire and a cap to match. It was the kind of attire that Bernie Grant, MP had begun to wear at recent state openings of the British Parliament, only this was much more sophisticated and fitted the giant of a man better. He was full of life, and he was talking with her.

"There goes my dream," Chrys mumbled to himself.

The Tandy brought him back to reality. A female voice was saying something. He continued his approach, hoping that by the time he reached her, the man would have disappeared. Like the proverbial four monkeys, he would see nothing, hear nothing, say nothing, and do nothing.

Using the knife as a screw driver, Chrys set about unscrewing the small screws from the bracket, which had disengaged itself due to excessive stress. He relieved the bag of some contents, and screwed back the bracket. The mystery mademoiselle and the mystery man were still engaged in a hearty discussion. It was obvious they knew each other. Curiosity overwhelmed Chrys, and he trained his ear to their conversation. They were speaking in Hausa, a major Nigerian language also spoken in some sub-Saharan, West African nations.

He eased himself out of the vicinity and headed to the nearest bar for a pint of lager. Half way through the second pint, somebody tapped him on the shoulder. Chrys looked up and saw a follicle-challenged, oriental gentleman pointing in the direction from whence he had come. She was waving and beckoning him to come back. The man in *agbada* had disappeared.

The airport formalities were smooth. They had little time for the duty-free shopping, but he managed to buy a few things while she went to the ladies: a personal stereo cassette player/recorder, some drinks, fags, five bottles of Poison perfume, chocolates, etc.

Chrys used his phone card to call Ossie.

"Ol' boy, how come you left without telling me?"

"What do you mean?" That meant Chrys didn't intend to explain. Responding to a question with another question was a typical Nigerian conversational tool for avoiding a direct answer. They talked briefly; Chrys had no time to kill. "Thanks for everything."

"It's okay," Ossie sounded pleased. "Oh, your landlady called. She said a recorded package came in this morning for you."

"Thanks. Tell Jackie I wish her the merriest Christmas ever, whenever she comes out of the solitary confinement! Bye." He dropped before Ossie could put in another word. He dialled 0703 and Ivy's number.

"Let's go," she said sexily as he retrieved his card.

"After you, Ma'am!" His head was in the clouds of an outer galaxy.

Inside the plane, Chrys put away their hand luggage in the overhead locker. He kept the shopping with him, since it contained some items they might need as the six-hour flight progressed.

"And what might these things be?" she asked.

"You'll find out if, when, and as the need arises."

"I want to see them now." Her green eye glowed like some liquid crystals had been injected into it.

"No, you won't."

"Oh yes, I will." She looked convincingly determined.

"Oh no, you won't," Chrys crowed as in pantomimes.

She went for the bag. Chrys tried to prevent her from seeing the contents. The man seated on the next row didn't seem to mind their childish pranks, but the pilot was welcoming passengers to BA Flight 075 from London Gatwick to Murtala Muhammed Airport, Lagos. He let her.

She went through the bag's content. He ignored her. The pilot rambled on about the flight details and what the weathermen had said about clouds and turbulence over the Sahara.

"So you smoke these?"

"No." He didn't smoke mentholated cigarettes.

"If you don't, who does? She shoved one roll of St Moritz under his nose.

"You do." Chrys could easily decipher the probing questions as her triumph over capturing the bag translated into a defeat: Her eyes dimmed and she looked beaten. He continued, "How did I know you smoke? How did I know the brand? And Gordon Gin, how did I know that too? Black coffee, eh? I should have known you were a naughty girl."

"You snoopy son of a spy," she said jokingly, colour returning to her misty eyes.

5

She was leaning on him as she nibbled at a piece of chocolate. Chrys was thrilled watching her so happy and behaving as if he was a long-lost loving uncle who had suddenly turned up in her life when she needed him.

He wondered what sort of woman sat with him. He had seen them all, he thought, and he categorised them into four distinct groups: Jennifer, Jacinta, Jackie, and Janet. Jennifer Body goes out and gets what she wants; she does not believe in destiny. She dreams and makes her dreams come true. Jennifer walks while her age-graders crawl; she flies when they walk. The Igbo concept of *Chi*, or personal providence, piloting human affairs holds little water for her; Chi must follow the pace she dictates. She makes men sit up and take notice. The fact that she is reincarnated biblical Delilah deters no man from plunging into her fantasy world in the land of lady tarantulas.

Jacinta Soul plays it by the ears and reacts differently to different stimuli. A believer in family virtues and old-fashioned fidelity, she is the modern Catherine of Aragon and represents a larger spectrum of the human female species. Life outside matrimony is scary. She dwells on sentimental constraints and hindsight concerns.

Jackie Mind has had her hay days, but she knows where her bread is better buttered. She does not pay the pipers, yet she dictates the tune. She wants to have it all, but she won't step up to the plate and make matters move to a desired direction. Specialists in frozen feelings and in pulling background strings, the vortex of their anger could uproot an iroko tree.

Janet Heart has wild streaks but, in the right hands, she makes mankind proud of its female species. Her smiling fine face is a mask; she could be anything deep down in her heart.

Chrys wondered where to place the lady sitting by his side. Fatima—if that was her name—should be pious, pretty, and religious; religious in the Catholic as well as in the Islamic faith. In the latter, she was the daughter of a prophet; in the former, the Portuguese town where Our Lady Madonna showed up. He settled on Janet because her name did not quite unmask her.

The "No Smoking" sign had gone off, but the "Fasten Your Seat Belt" sign still glowed. The plane was safely in the air and slowly edging to the cruising height.

"Hey, remember me?"

It dawned on Chrys that they hadn't actually introduced themselves. He was about to remedy that when a stewardess leaned over to ask what they would like to drink. They both settled for orange juice. He gulped down the misery quota, forgoing the snack that accompanied the drink. "Where are we?"

"What are you called?" she asked.

"I'm Chimé, Chiké Chimé," he said in a Bond, James Bond fashion.

"Enugu area?"

"Kene community, specifically," he volunteered. He was surprised and looked it.

"I thought as much. Pleased to meet you," she said, offering her hand with the palm covering his already outstretched palm.

Her hand was supple. The long, glossy fingernails formed a perfect geometrical curve. It was simply irresistible. Chrys raised it to his lips, as conveniently as the sitting arrangement could allow, and kissed it.

"Ooh là là! Enchanté. A gentleman too!"

It is un-African to kiss a woman's hand, and the custom was out of fashion in Britain, but he thought he was dealing with someone who would appreciate a romantic remnant of his Latin days. "Do you mind?

"No. It's just that nobody has ever kissed my hand."

"I am honoured. Now, let me guess: You are Fatima."

"We have established that; just don't call me 'Fatty' or 'Fati.'"

"Your surname, or rather your father's name, is Mohammed?" It was more of a question than a statement of fact. In fact, he was only trying to impress her with his knowledge of world religions.

"How did you know that?" she demanded.

"May I continue?" He had nothing else to add; he was playing mind games.

"No, first tell me how you knew my surname is Mohammed."

Chrys was not going to tell; he didn't know. "Let me finish first."

"Okay, you recognized the General," she concluded.

"What General?" he asked as if he was feigning ignorance.

"Come on, you were pretending all the time that you did not recognize General Sarkin-Mohammed; retired, of course."

****

General Garba Abdullahi Sarkin-Mohammed, a veteran of the Nigeria-Biafra War, played important roles during General Murtala Muhammed leadership interlude. In a wide-ranging reorganization in 1978, before General Olusegun Obasanjo's regime left the scene, Garba was promoted Major General and posted to purely military duties. Those who remained in government were to retire as soon as the transition was completed.

When the military handed over power in 1979, President Shehu Shagari reviewed the role of the "khaki boys"—as military men are called. It was generally agreed that the threat of a military putsch persisted for as long as some hotheads were left in the barracks. With the help of service chiefs, who had jumped into the political bed with the "*agbada* men," as politicians are called, those suspected of a high propensity to strike were promoted and retired. General Garba was prominent among those retired.

The last time anybody read anything official about him, he was photographed queuing up in the London School of Economics refectory. He had registered for a postgraduate programme. He was soon forgotten as the cocktail of corruption and criminality coached the 1990s flimflam frauds, the so-called "419-ners" who preyed on the gullible worldwide. With the listening regime of General Ibrahim B. Babangida in its fifth year and preparing to launch "the doomed days of democracy," Garba appeared to have gone the way of many before him: rich retirement and background influence-peddling.

****

Chrys knew Nigerian politics like the lines on his palm. Army officers did not normally marry foreigners. General Garba was right in the centre of controversies; a newspaper should have established the European connection. He didn't think he was with the daughter of the larger-than-life General Garba: the cat with nine lives; the man who went to the guillotine and came back smiling; the man who dined with kings, defaced the palace walls, and lived to tell the story. However, he knew he was playing with fire.

Convinced that the lady was not for him, he asked, "Which one of the fat cats is your husband?"

"Get out of here!"

"I can't—it's a long way down," Chrys noted and pointed out of the window as if to remind her they were

33

thousands of feet above any solid or consistent liquid substance.

She looked out of the window, smiled, and sat back.

Chrys had lived long enough to know that the lady he sat with had all the hallmarks of a modern mess-not-with wife or mistress. According to a popular story from street rumour mills, a journalist was invited to a lavish state-house party for a visiting dignitary. He reportedly asked the wife of a kingpin for a dance. They had been friends and actually hailed from the same town. It was a straightforward dance: no frills, no lambada, no touching, and no blues—just a simple boogie-boogie woogie-woogie, smiles, and small talks about their one-eyed town where the same thing happened every four days.

The next time the journalist heard a human voice, they belonged to city council workers. Some overzealous security men had left him for dead in a waste heap 25 miles from where he sipped champagne hours before. The government flew him abroad for medical treatment. And the man died. Judicial inquiry followed. Six months and thousands of naira later, the panel submitted its findings. Another one year of government deliberations, the white paper appeared: USA—Unknown Security Agents. Case closed.

People steered clear of the big league, if they didn't belong there. Not only was he admiring the lady he knew nothing about, they were getting pretty close. He fancied her a lot and detected that she fancied him more than she was prepared to show. However, he didn't fancy his decaying body in some shallow and unmarked grave far away from the land that gave him life. Only a tree stands in the face of a roaring chainsaw.

6

"You want to give somebody cancer?" he asked her. She nodded. "Go ahead."

While she was gone, Chrys opened a bottle of wine and tuned his headset into a music channel. *Dick Tracy* was showing when she came back. Starring Warren Beatty and Ms. Louise (Madonna) Ciccone as "Breathless Mahoney," the promotion did not match reality; then again, Hollywood is all about hype. She placed her head on his shoulder to create more room for her long legs.

"Say, who was the guy who dropped you off? Your boyfriend?"

"Shouldn't that be my *toy boy*?"

"You tell me."

"Sean is a first cousin."

"Oh!" he sounded hollow and defeated.

"Oh? You don't seem convinced." She looked up.

Chrys changed course. "Your uncle, he lives in London?"

"Yes, he is a producer with BBC."

"Oh, I see; he's your Uncle from Auntie?"

"That's not funny," she snapped.

"I do not mean 'aunt,' as in your mom's sister; I mean the BBC: the TV Auntie."

She got the pun and managed a smile.

Chrys had come to terms with the fact that she was of Anglo-Nigerian decent, but he still couldn't place her: a plain Jennifer, just a Jacinta, a half-baked feminist Jackie, a liberal-minded Janet, or just an easygoing, spoilt daughter of a rich, retired army general and an Irish colleen.

She opened her eyes abruptly. "What is it, Chike?" She sat up.

35

This was the first time she called Chrys by name. He was touched; it was as if he just had a mental massage. "Nothing... I just did not think you were a Nigerian of...."

"Mixed race... half-caste or half-bred?"

"I don't use such terms. They don't feature in my vocabulary. There is only one race: the human race. The 'half' or 'mixed' concept I, therefore, find fundamentally flawed."

"I got that. So what were you going to say?"

"I was going to say 'of multicultural background.'"

"Ha!" she blurted. "That's a euphemistic crap. It makes sense, but that's not the way it is."

"That's the way it should be. The daughter of a Saxon and a Semite is not called 'half-bred,' neither are other intercontinental 'mixes'? Okay, you say *mulatto...* sorry, *mulattress*, but what does the word mean? I will tell you: It is Spanish for 'young mule.' We do not have to stick to crude conceptions just because it has been so since Adam and Eve. It's arrant nonsense, and it's time we got it right."

"I never thought of it that way. The problem is that you can't change an established nomenclature overnight."

"Says who? Examples abound. When previously innocent words become offensive to a section of the population, people adjust accordingly. We are talking about a living language, not one the Pharaohs spoke. A few years back, 'gay' meant something else. If one was called Richard, he told everybody, 'My friends call me Dick.' Today, it's Chad, Chas, Ritchie, etc. If we must give names, we might as well make them relate to peoples and places: African-American, for example."

"I get the impression that you have strong feelings about the subject."

"Yes," Chrys replied without really thinking about it.

"Why?"

"Well, let us say that I have had the opportunity to think about it." He did not want to tell her yet that he had a daughter of multicultural background.

It was quiet inside the plane. Passengers were taking their turns to ease off metabolic wastes. Occasional turbulence interrupted the thrust of the metallic contraption. He wouldn't want to wake her up even if he felt pressed. He did not feel like smoking. He wished she did not smoke; he would have given up at last. He had cut down drastically as part of his last birthday resolution and hoped to ditch the habit before New Year Day. In any case, he was not going to smoke at home. It was taboo in his family, and there was no compromise. His mother hated smoking, beards and moustaches, and drunks.

She stirred and opened her eyes.

"Are you all right?" Chrys asked. She nodded. "Say how come you are not spending Christmas with your folks in England?"

"I have part of my family in Nigeria. My sister...."

"Loretta?" She looked at him with disbelief in her eyes. "I overheard Sean at Victoria."

"Eavesdropping Eric! Now, tell me about you."

"What exactly would you want to know about me?"

She sat up, readjusted her glasses, and straightened her gold necklace. "Okay, it was not your wife that dropped you off at Victoria?" Chrys was surprised and looked it. She physically turned his face towards her. "Sing me a song, sunshine, and make it top-ten."

"No, you go on guessing."

"Okay, maybe it would help your brain to formulate a decent lie I can swallow. The chick is definitely of Afro-Caribbean origin."

"Holy Milingo!"

"Stop swearing with the archbishop's name," she cautioned Chrys.

He was surprised that she knew about the Archbishop of Lusaka, Zambia, who was *under observation* at the Vatican. "She is not my wife; 'Nessa is a cousin-in-law."

"So, are you married?" she asked.

"No."

"That was quick," she remarked.

"You?"

"No, I am not married, fortunately."

"I'll second that."

"Obviously, you are not gay."

"No," he assured her. "However, if I were gay, I would give it up for you! No, that's something I don't understand."

"Have you had time to think about it?"

"Yes, and I am not convinced that homosexuality comes from creation; it is a choice. It has nothing to do with my culture or nurture. I just cannot comfortably picture an intercourse of such sexual shade."

"Doesn't that make you homophobic?"

"I am most definitely not," Chrys protested.

"There is nothing unnatural about homosexuality. I am convinced that somehow.... Let me finish," she insisted as he tried to interject. "You see, it must take more than the environment to breed the large army of gays and lesbians. If the biological base could be ascertained, I believe that the tag of 'social aberration' would fade away."

"Bulls! That's a part of the loads of bovine scatology and pseudo-psychiatric nonsense making rounds in academia. Ever heard of the concept of critical mass? Next, some sick boffin will tell us that paedophilia comes naturally. Well, I don't think man is designed to prefer

38

men to women. I may be wrong but, until I know better, that's how it stays."

"And woman-to-woman?" she asked.

"I don't see the good sides of it either. Here, however, I tend to be partial. Sincerely speaking, I don't care who sleeps with whom, and I don't see why we should be told. Okay, I'm a bit more comfortable with lesbianism."

"I'm not surprised. The male acceptance of *ménage a trois* makes that pretty obvious."

Chrys smiled and said, "The truth of the matter is that during our secondary school days, nobody frowned at college pseudo-lesbianism, or the society pretended it didn't exist."

"*Supé?*"

"Yes, '*supé*' is presently equated to lesbianism, but it was not in origin. It did not extend to two mature women because our society does not accept the concept. *Supé* was a phase in a teenage girl's growth, an unstructured mentoring programme. You went to high school in Nigeria?" She nodded. "During my time, well over half of the girls in girls-only schools must have experimented, and over 90% were not sexual. It was a sort of one-on-one tutorial whereby the older took the younger through such essentials of life as menstruation, mouth-to-mouth kissing, meeting and dating boys, et cetera. It faded and phased out as the girls matured, married, and multiplied. As you know, many mothers did not discuss such issues with their daughters and sex education was zilch. No, *supé* has had its day. Satellite television now rules."

"So what are you doing in England?" she asked to change the subject.

"Adult education."

"Where?"

"Southampton-on-Solent," Chrys informed her. Actually, the city sat on the beds of Rivers Itchen and Test.

"Lovely place, I heard. Sean's girlfriend is there. Are you on scholarship or something?"

"Sort of, and my old man subsidizes the academic wanderlust."

"You are a thoughtful and romantic man, you know?"

"You're referring to the nosegay and all?"

"Yes, and calling Ivy and Kylie before boarding and all."

"Holy Milingo! Ivy is my landlady. Kylie is a pussycat. You Eavesdropping Erika! I called to check on a piece of mail that arrived after I had left."

"Wasn't it important?"

"No. It was a rejection letter from a publisher I had sent synopsis of a book on African dictators."

"You write?"

"I dabble. It keeps me away from clubbing and...."

"Mischief?"

"Do I look mischievous? No, something happened and I needed to lay it on somebody."

"What is the title?" she asked.

"*The Wacky World of Dark Dictators*," he offered.

"Sounds like double trouble to me."

Chrys had not even given a thought to the title. She was bringing out the best in him. He was impressed with himself and quickly made a mental note of the tentative title, *Wacky World*.

The lights came on. Six hours gone. A crewmember gave the usual instructions, mainly for foreigners. *Foreigners* had a certain strange ring. He felt a few inches taller.

"Come on, stranger!" Chrys said. She did not get the joke, but she smiled.

The exit tube took awhile to fix. When the door opened, it took another long wait to get to it.

Chrys carried the bulk of the hand luggage. He had picked up, packed, and sorted out their bits and pieces to ease eventual separation. They walked side by side down the tube. Right at the end of the straight stretch stood a soldier with a placard that read: "AMANDA."

Chrys grinned but said nothing until they were in line for immigration formalities. "The Chairman of the 'Anglo Moms and Naijâ Dads Association' must have been on board," Chrys wisecracked and chuckled.

"That would have been very funny if it weren't so pathetic," she blurted, then took her bag and moved away from him.

Chrys felt embarrassed. Like a sweet dream, it had come to an end. He had done it before; he just did it again: put his foot in his mouth. Only Chrys in the whole wide world could call his wife "Gypsy Girl" when she isn't one. Even when she objected, he still called her "Gee Girl." Only Chrys could tell a girlfriend, who isn't well-endowed with a chest-full of fleshy treasures, that silicone would do wonders for her. Only Chrys could unravel an abbreviation so cannily for someone who had a Nigerian father and a British mother. *Some Silly Sayings of Chrys Chiké Chimé* would be a bestseller.

Airport formalities over, Chrys came out to see a multicoloured multitude of people welcoming loved ones. The soldier with the placard had moved post past the Customs gate and still waited.

"Chiké!" a female from the crowd screamed. Maggie, his elder sister, embraced and hung onto him for some time.

Chrys and Kevin, her husband, pumped hands hard and made intricate finger movements, the way only the well-acquainted did. "Brother Kev, thanks for coming out this night."

"Nonsense," Kevin said. "We wouldn't...." He stopped suddenly and looked askance at his wife. Maggie shrugged and wore a rather hostile countenance.

Chrys followed their eyes, and there she was.

"May I share your trolley, sir?" she said, grinning from ear to ear.

"Oh… please meet my sister, Mrs. Margaret Tagboo, and her husband Kevin. Maggie, Kev, meet...."

"Adaeze," she cut in. "Happy to meet you both."

"Welcome, Princess. Please call me Kev; everybody does."

Maggie gave Kevin a reprimanding look. She embraced Chrys's companion as was the custom amongst women, but it was not warm. Maggie never took easily to strangers, and her reluctance did not surprise Chrys for obvious reasons.

If Maggie was surprised, Chrys was dumbfounded. Adaeze? The name explained a lot of things. To use her word, she was probably "double trouble."

Maggie pulled him aside and let Kevin move on with the lady. "Chiké, when are you going to learn? You want to make everybody's Christmas a misery again?"

"Sister," Chrys cut in, sounding as affectionate as possible. "You will understand when I tell you the whole story."

"How do you expect me to understand when you hook up with these *oyibo* women?"

"I did not sit through the ordeal of a six-hour flight to talk about that. And she is not 'white,' woman; damn it. Shall we go?"

She wrestled the briefcase from him and matched on. She stopped suddenly and said, "I thought you and Ebere Onaga were serious?"

Chrys ignored her. Maggie was getting on his nerves. His relationship with Jackie was none of her business. He walked past her into the dimly lit car park. It was clear that Gina-era prejudices still clouded Maggie's judgement. Even then, she never gave Gina, his ex, a chance.

Kevin and Adaeze were already seated in the Peugeot 505 Evolution and chatting as though they had known each other since before the war. Maggie opened the owner's corner, entered, and slammed the door hard. Chrys quietly sat behind the driver, beside his simmering sister. The soldier with the placard came running towards them. Kevin told him to move on, that there was nothing else they could do. "Fasten your seat belts. I'll be cruising at an average of 100 kilometres an hour as soon as we hit the expressway. Our next stop will be the V. I. Carport."

Kevin cruised at over the speed he had promised, thanks to the military Land Rover with two soldiers. They arrived at the 1004 Flats, Victoria Island. Kevin dismissed the escort soldiers with enough money to cover a carton of beer.

Chrys wanted to know whom they owed the honour of an armed escort from the airport. It was Colonel Omar Idris, Kevin's brother-in-law. They had a baby boy, and there was a party at their Ikoyi residence. "He received a phone call from a superior in London that an Amanda was coming in with that flight. Since he, Omar, couldn't get away, he sent the two men. He said her father has a house here in V. I. We agreed to give her a ride while the soldiers carried the luggage. She must have done an abracadabra. So, how's London?"

"It has hardly changed much since the Romans left."

He ignored Chrys's cheap crack and asked directly, "How are Ossie and family?"

"They send their regards."

Kevin talked as they waited for "Princess" to come down. She came down dressed in a two-tone, black-grey dress in stretch jersey with long sleeves and a fashionable court shoe, lined with foam-backed fabric. On her neck dangled an "A"-initial pendant on 16-inch chain with matching earrings. On her wrist, she wore a solid-gold, ridged-effect bangle. She sat besides Chrys. The Poison perfume was unadulterated by cigarette smoke or alcohol. She was offered a bottle of beer. She wanted something soft, ginger ale or soda water.

Kevin couldn't wait, as soon as Maggie and the princess retired, to turn the discussion to where he wanted it. Everything Chrys said fell on deaf ears, including the possibility that she might be somebody's wife.

"Ignorance can be bliss. What you do not know won't hurt you. It's not everyday that fresh-stream eels are sold at Ojuelegba Market. And if you want my advice...."

"I don't! Kev, please, let's adjourn; I'm knackered."

"You are knack-what?"

"Tired," Chrys explained. "I am too tired to coordinate the functioning of my milk monitor, my bloody brain."

"Okay, I give up. It seems the leopard has changed its spots. I would never have believed the cold of England could wreak so much havoc on a child of Chimé."

"And don't you go blabbing to Maggie." Chrys completely ignored his obscene innuendoes.

"Men do not sell each other down the River Eve."

Chrys turned on his side and slept off almost immediately.

His nephew and nieces were all over him within hours. Maggie was back from morning Mass, and breakfast would be ready in a few minutes. As if on cue, Adaeze emerged.

"Good morning, Chiké, I am going to jog; are you coming?"

"Good morning. I really don't know a thing about this island," Chrys confessed.

"Don't worry; I am *diana* around these parts."

Dee-ahnah? The pronunciation of the word was definitely Enugu-Onitsha, Igbo urban dialect. The so-called southern Igbo would use "*diala*." To say that she was not a stranger to the island, the word "*amaala*" would be more appropriate in central Igbo. "*Diana*" or "*diala*" is an exclusive male title in some parts of Igboland, meaning "freeborn" or "master of the land" or, to be more linguistically hip, "son of the soil." A female version of the lexical item would be "*adaana*," which had no spoken significance.

Bar Beach held unpleasant memories. The first thing Chrys associated with the place was public execution of condemned armed robbers. This morning, spiritual churchgoers in their robes of different shades bunched together in worship. White- and red-robed religious rebels walked about on ten-toes.

They sat down on a lonely part of the beach, the wild sea storm and sea-to-land breeze pushing away the music and chants of Charismatic Catholicism and Pentecostal Protestantism. She held Chrys by the arm and said, "I think we need to talk."

"Shoot," he urged her.

"No, you shoot."

"Why did you claim to be Fatima?"

"I didn't; you assumed I was Fatima."

45

"Okay, is General Garba your father?"

"He is not my father."

"So you are Eze's daughter?" She nodded. "Why concatenate… compound it?"

"It's en vogue: Madonna, Latifah, Sinitra, Prince, Sade, Cher, Anya...?"

"Well, it's not customary...." Chrys began to say.

"I just like it. Adaeze: Princess."

Every girl in every Igbo family is *ada* (daughter); it does not necessarily have to be the first girl. Adaeze is quite common, so are the following: Adaobi, Adaora, Adaoma, Adamma, or other peculiar dialectical combinations. The name "Eze" (king) is about the commonest pan-Igbo name, even though the Igbo as a nation had no king.

To change the subject, she said, "Tell me how you came about a broken marriage so early."

"My dear, I'm not a spring chicken...."

"No, but you are not a good specimen of Methuselah either."

They both laughed. She tilted her head lovey-dovey until it came to rest on his shoulder. Chrys picked some stones, seven of them. He threw them towards the raging ocean one after the other. It was not meant to signify anything, but seven was his lucky number.

"Now, tell me about your marriage?"

"Broken marriage," Chrys corrected. "There's not much to say. I got involved and, without the usual family support, it hit the rocks."

"And Kelem is the product?"

"K. L. M.—Kamemena Lucia Maria. How did you know that?"

"I overheard the children. The maid apparently led them to believe that I was Auntie Gina. The boy bet his lunch coke that Gina wouldn't breeze into town 'without

Kelem because Uncle Chiké will show her pepper.' Those were his exact words."

"Holy Milingo! How did he get the idea?" He knew. Domestic disputes with Gina were mostly public and widely reported. And when the nanny goat chews its cud, the kids watch.

8

Chrys squeezed out more information; yet, somehow, he still doubted her name. Her family included an only boy, Charles, who was in the United States, and three other girls: Loretta, who was living in Enugu, and Britain-based twins, Mary and Martha.

"Well, mine is a bit bigger... larger. Maggie is my immediate senior. There's a brother before her, Michael. Anthony follows me; twins Patrick and Patricia follow, and Nneka brings the rear."

They left Lagos on Tuesday. The airport lounge was a motley market of mostly sweating black bodies clad in a rainbow of garments. A Nigeria Airways plane sat on the tarmac. Chrys refused to travel on scalper or backyard-business tickets, which were almost double the going rate; it was not the money, but the principle. She would not fly the notoriously noisy private shuttle. She walked over to the Airport Manager's office. Within minutes, she came back waving two tickets.

"That is a display of flagrant favouritism," Chrys commented. "I hope your conscience doesn't break your heart."

"My friend, get real; this is not Cloud Chiké-land." No heads turned. No one minded her display of the art of man-know-man; everybody was talking at the same time. "Let's get out of this oven."

The plane looked like the inside of a coach that had seen better days. The 50-minute flight was smooth, and the landing was excellent.

The taxi from Enugu Airport went through the new access road called IBB Way. The driver observed that it had been named after the military president. Chrys did not want to talk local politics. He was considering his companion's proposal that they should spend some time together to get to know each other better.

As soon as they checked into Nike Lake Resort Hotel, Chrys contributed to the debate. "I think that driver made some sense. An active public functionary, especially the chief executive, should not allow sycophantic subordinates to name infrastructures after him. Don't get me wrong, I have nothing against benevolent dictatorship but, as devoted democrats, personal occultism and hero-worshipping are alien to Igbo rugged republicanism."

She looked up and said, "Do you mind saying that in English!"

They had lunch in the hotel's open-space restaurant. She insisted on picking the bill and left a big tip, which Chrys found quite out of proportion and said so. The waiter's week was made, and it was "Madam, Madam" thereafter. After lunch, they made their way back to their room. He held her by the waist with his left hand and crossed her right hand round his waist. He opened the door and walked in first, as if to inspect it. The room smelled of humid harmattan.

"You had a nice day, Ma'am? Any tips left, Ma'am?"

"Don't you start, Signor Stingy!"

As she walked past him, Chrys held her firmly by the waist. Her resistance was mild. He held her and looked into her eyes; she, into his. They looked at each other for what seemed like eternity. He pecked her lightly on the inviting, chunky lips. She closed her eyes, pouted, and parted her lips. Chrys let her wait while he gave her a little bite on the neck. Her fire of passion was lit. She held him and located his mouth without opening her eyes. She kissed him passionately, their noses partially blocked and exhaling into each other's nostrils.

He began to undress her. She did not mind. His hands wandered off to more private places. She did not mind. "Erm… mm," his voice muffled, "the door is open."

She stopped suddenly, stepped out of her dress, and looked at him as if she was seeing him for the first time. Like a wounded tigress, her pose was awesome. She was wearing an unpadded, front-opening designer bra, and the pair of matching *broderie-anglaise* briefs was breathtaking on her. "Go on," she commanded. "Close the bloody door before someone sees us and tells the town crier."

"Don't be silly. I was only thinking…."

"*Thinking!* Don't you have any sense of spontaneity, a desire for adventure?"

She was fuming as Chrys considered how best to cage her. She was still breathing heavily and not bothering to pick up her summer-perfect beach dress. Like a man possessed, he ripped open his shirt—separating all the buttons in the process.

"Okay baby, let's have an African adventure; my sense of spontaneity runneth over!"

She smiled and stood her ground. Chrys wrapped his arms around her and kissed her intensely. He undid the whalebone fastening, which yielded as though it was waiting for him to touch it. A chance touch of her mammary nodes, she twitched as if an electric current passed through her. He moved his hands up and down her trunk as if to soften her. Slowly, he negotiated the progress of his fingers and touched her. Her knees wobbled, and her head went into a slight spin.

As he lowered her gently on the fluffy floor, her shoes walked away. Before she could spell "spontaneity," she was in her birthday suit. All of a sudden, she pulled away, stood up, and ran into the bathroom.

"What's up, Tigress? Did you keep your *spontaneity* there?"

"Chiké," she said from behind the bathroom door, "be a sport and close that door. There is a time and there is a place for every activity known to humans. We cannot both be mad at the same time."

"Speak for yourself. The door remains open until we both burn out our spirit of spontaneity."

"Suit yourself. I am not coming out of here until you do."

Chrys needed no further prompting to change his stand. The mood was too good to forfeit to pig-headed pomposity. He slammed the door so hard it shook the walls. She appeared from the bathroom with a towel tied round her bosom and showing all her limbs. As Chrys stood there looking at the credible creature, she walked past him, drew the curtains, and switched on the air-condition unit full blast.

"Tara!" she shrieked as she ripped off the towel and jumped into bed. "This is the place, the altar of Venus."

It sounded sacrilegious, but Chrys couldn't be bothered at the moment. He was not going to wait for a formal invitation. Her body outline was like that of reedbuck, Africa's most gracious gazelle. Every piece of flesh was in its rightful place, baby-bum soft, super supple, and glowing gold. Her unbridled treasures assumed a breathtaking prominence on the svelte work of divine design. With his lissom and luscious lips stimulated, Chrys could not decide where best to start. Seeing her whole body, as God made it three decades before, he began to feast on it.

The haloed hips gave the final destination the aura of a golden port of Greek gods, where only the divinely selected dared to anchor. Nothing would stop him from docking, not even the anger of gods; no, not then. In his traditional Igbo religion, *Ọdịnanị*, that was A-class foolishness because there are many deities to placate individually with offerings. He was offering his soul, his mind, his heart, and his body—his being—to all of them. Born and brought up a Catholic, he felt there wasn't a sin that confession couldn't clean and that a sin shared was a sin half-forgiven. His head held high, he stayed the course.

They were too tired to talk about it, a deep departure from Jackie's intellectualisation of sex. Four hours later, he woke up, picked up the quilt from his own side of the bed, and covered her. She felt the warmth and opened her eyes, groaned with undisguised solicitude, and smiled.

"Come here," she said sweetly. As he bent over to kiss her, she grabbed him with more force than Chrys could have credited her. "Go ahead, *kill* me!" No more words were needed, no embrace excluded, and no sensor spared. She no longer sweated small stuff; someone was making her his queen.

They checked out before ten on the third day. Hotel shuttle was nonexistent. Out of the hazy harmattan sunshine, an inner-city cab crawled into view. A blot, it became more so as it pulled in from the gate, against the expanse environment of the five-star hotel with its gardens and serene lake. It wore a recent painting of bright yellow and black top. From the distance, it looked like any other Peugeot 504 assembled in Nigeria: big, bold headlamps, four troublesome doors, and a front that reflected possible Citroën ancestry. The taxi rattled and swayed as it approached. The valves needed setting. The ignition timing was screaming to be synchronized. The tail pipe was tap-dancing to the discordant rap music from the whistling fan belt and drumming engine exhaust system, half of which was visible from the elevated hotel foyer.

A dashing, dusky damsel dressed in a chic yuppie suit alighted and walked past them, leaving a trail of cheap shouting perfume, cheapened further by the wetness of her month-old Jerry Curls perm. As they settled into the taxi, the driver let the engine get more fuel and, assured that it had attained steady-state combustion, he proceeded to the take-off preliminaries. The strong stench of the engine exhaust emissions was overpowering.

Approaching Abakaliki Road, the driver demanded to know their destination.

"Chimé Close, New Haven."

She looked at him and asked: "Are you sure your folks won't mind?"

"My mother may be a little not-too-enthusiastic, but she is a nice lady."

"Aren't all mothers? Sometimes, it is as if they jostle for position with their sons' lovers. Fathers generally don't mind." She was right, but no one had said they were lovers.

His mother was not home; she had travelled to the village for Christmas, his baby-sister Nneka informed them. He decided to see his father at his Zik Avenue office to arrange for a car. He had no interest in the family real estate business nor in the ageing transport wing. Michael was running the show as if it was his basic birthright. All Chrys wanted was to teach college courses and to write.

He knocked lightly on the door, and walked into the spacious office. His father sat behind a large executive table. The name label, "CHIEF (SIR) PATRICK CHUKWUKA CHIMÉ, KSM," had been redesigned to take in a new chieftaincy title and his knighthood of St. Mulumba.

"My friend!" Chief Chimé exclaimed. "Where have you been?"

"Hello, Papa."

"Come here!" He opened his arms and Chrys fell in between them. "Welcome, my friend. Where is the person I heard about? Maggie called to warn us the night you arrived. She said you were taking some Gina-type lady to Kaduna for a few days."

"Huh?"

"So, what happened? Is she any good?" Chrys went to the door and beckoned her to come in. "Welcome, my daughter," Chief Chimé said before Chrys could introduce her.

"Greetings to you, Chief, Sir," she said genuflecting and bowing at the same time.

"Please stop bowing to me; I am not God. We Ndiigbo do not prostrate before humans because all powers belong to *Chineke*, the Creator." It was obvious that Maggie, blinded by prejudice, did not elaborate. She simply drew a tangent to Gina, like running scared of a housefly long after an aerial attack by a disoriented African killer bee. "You look very familiar. Who is your father?" Chief Chimé asked pointedly.

"Typical! How would he know her father?" Chrys wondered.

"Chief Anthony Chukwuemeka Arinze, Sir," she said lowering her eyes.

"Emeka Arinze! I was with him last Saturday at the Sports Club. Wait, let me guess: You are the Ada of yesterday?" She nodded respectfully, looking up and dropping her eyes again. "Come here, come... come...." He held her to his body like a big baby. "Remember when I came with my friend, your Uncle Cletus, to visit you at QRC?" She nodded. "How's your mother, Susan?"

"She is okay."

"And your sister... Mandy?"

"Mary," she corrected. "I am Amanda."

"True talk! Amanda, yes; I remember now, but we called you Adaeze.... Chiké, why didn't you tell me? She is your *sister*."

9

Amanda Arinze! Chrys was speechless; his eyes, empty. He had heard so much about her. He had even seen her teenage-years photos, but they had never met.

He listened as she and his father relived the past. He gathered the gist: Amanda was understandably picked on at school because she was an easy target. First, she was very conspicuous. Obviously, she spoke better English and with a *foreign* accent. She had rich parents, a wealthy and famous grandfather, and an uncle in the corridors of power. Garba, then a brigadier, didn't make things any easier. He would show up whenever he felt like it with a platoon of combat-ready soldiers. Then there was the twice-a-year visit to England. Those who weren't allowed in her circle became mini-monsters.

When Garba left for a short course at Camberly, England, the bigger girls closed in. A second cousin in the same school informed her father, Cletus Onaga, then a state high court judge. The lawman told his friend Patrick Chimé, a wealthy businessman. They travelled to the Holy Rosary College, Nsukka to prevail on the reverend-mother principal to put a stop to the harassment. The godly lady did, but Amanda did not particularly like the intervention. It created a running rift with the second cousin and revived an old and unnecessary family feud.

"Of course, you know that your father's long arms grabbed my secretary, Amaka."

"Dad!" Chrys cautioned.

"Oh, I didn't realize you were not aware...."

"It's all right, Uncle, I've heard all about it," Amanda admitted, using a respectful term for elderly male friends of one's family.

Chrys coughed uneasily to stop his father from going over uncharted terrains.

"Okay! Nneka said you were coming over for a car."

"Don't your daughters have anything better to do?" Chrys wondered.

"I demand to be informed. Now, please take my daughter Amanda to see her father before he disappears to Abuja. Here, take the key."

They drove off in an old but well-conditioned Peugeot 504.

"Okay, Miss No-more-a-mystery, what is General Garba to you?"

"He is my father's first cousin. My paternal Grandma Amina and his father, the Emir of Dualla, came down the same birth canal. Next question!"

"Why didn't you tell me?"

"I didn't know things were going to turn out this way."

He turned into Edinburgh Road, hoping to pick up a free route to Independence Layout through Presidential Road.

"Chrys, please go anywhere but the Chief's house."

"I didn't tell you to call me Chrys," he protested.

"I didn't tell you I am called Amanda," she retorted.

"Was that why you ignored the poor messengers at the Airport?" She smiled and said nothing. "So, your supervisor tagged your doctoral thesis 'anglosaxophobic nonsense,' huh?"

Amanda was startled. "How did you get that?"

"I'm going to give you brain tumour for all the white hairs you gave me these past days," he swore light-heartedly. "Something tells me our meeting was not

coincidental. And you had to throw my sister Maggie off
our trail with that Kaduna crap."

****

A lot of water passed under the bridge before
January 1991. Chrys's ex-wife Gina flew into town with
their daughter Kamemena. She raised some dust, but
nothing comparable to the first time she came to town.
Chrys and Amaka, who was sent to help them, had taken
the child and run home to Nigeria in 1983. They claimed
that Gina was an unfit mother. Gina came after them. She
came with Mario Monteneggro, the mighty muscleman of
Perugia's *capo de tutti capi*, with whom she lived after she
and Chrys had split.

For starters, Mario was deported. Gina vented her
Latin temper tantrum. She did not speak Igbo, and her
English was terrible. Folks said she was either mad or
dumb. Without warning, Chrys's father let her leave with
the child. Everybody was dumbfounded. It was
considered abomination; no agnate gives up its infant kin
in Igboland, no matter the crime. Conventional wisdom
dictated that the parable of the hawk and the hen applied
here. The hawk returned the chick of the hushed hen, not
that of the hell-raising hen. Notwithstanding her
perceived deficiencies and garrulity, Chief Chimé saw a
caring and protective mother who had crossed oceans
and deserts in search of her daughter.

****

Christmas Day, Gina came in peace. The wise
gesture of Chief Chimé was reciprocated. She handed the
child over to the man she still called "Papa." She spent a
week with the Chimés and left early in the New Year for
Canada. She was going into business with a lesbian
escort-agency madam whom Chrys called "a vegetarian
butcher." Gina left with Chief Arinze to Lagos; he was
headed to London. He and Gina got on well. Arinze was

not one to fail women. Chrys knew that Gina was getting even for what she called "calculated cruelty" in the early 80s, and Arinze was most willing to be used. Amaka, now Mrs. Arinze, stayed out of her way and Amanda's.

The main thing that brought Amanda home to her fatherland was sinister, to say the least. Her mother Sue had told her in a casual discussion that she only had to go down to the cellar in their Wimbledon house and she would write ten doctoral theses. She did and found stashed-away secret papers of Biafran Bureau of State Security (BOSS). She went to work and found out that her father was probably a double-agent. She told Mary, her sister. Mary might not have been the man's darling, but he fathered them. She told their aunt Patricia. Aunt Pat told her husband Seamus Kelly. Seamus alerted Arinze and Garba.

In a blind rage, Amanda was bent on "making my sperm-donor father know some pain." Her calculations did not foresee that she would become a social leper to many people, an outcast. Her determination to burst the dam also targeted the man for whom she had a baby while at the university. She considered it rape that the man, now Colonel Omar Idris, took advantage of her innocence and vulnerability.

Amanda wanted to burn down a palace to smoke out the two rats, but many princes and princesses would be homeless, including Garba. It didn't matter to her who got hurt, as long as her father was made to bite some dust for what she perceived he did to her, her mother, and her siblings, and as long as Omar was pulled down from his high horse. To label her father a wartime saboteur would have had disastrous effects on his political ambitions. Twenty years after the war, many people still felt very strongly about the Nigeria-Biafra War. Any serious political party would drop such a millstone or lose a big chunk of Igbo votes. She would then say that she got the information from Omar, who was at the State Security Services (SSS). The revelation would have ended his military career with immediate effect.

Garba confronted her at Gatwick, but he was not satisfied with her explanations. He called Omar to pick her up and shadow her, but the colonel was having a posh party; he sent his orderlies. By the time he realized the booboo, Amanda had left Lagos.

Chrys fell for her and understood why she set out to blaze the trail of hate: She needed a man in her life, or so he thought. After the festivities, Amanda warmed up a little to her father and accepted the idea that she had a stepmother, albeit illegal in English and Catholic canon laws, under which her parents were still married.

Early days of the New Year, Amanda's brother Charles zoomed into town with his African-American wife LeJeune. Arinze had to abort his London trip and set Gina adrift after a couple of days in Lagos. It provided the Chimés an opportunity to visit the Arinzes and to declare their intention by "knocking on the door," as if that was what brought them to town. In Igbo culture, that spelt "engagement" and a lifetime journey of matrimonial relationship. The traditional wedding was fixed for December 1991, midway between their birthdays and the first anniversary of their meeting.

Chrys summarized the events in his personalized, leather-bound, five-year diary. In conclusion, he wrote, "This is the magic of Amanda, the magic of all that is good and potentially bad rolled into one. The causal current is a family problem and should stay in the family. Money was never her motive in seeking to team up with the opposition party; she didn't even know their politics. The urge to see her father suffer a political setback was not sadistic; it was a classical case of blighted blues."

10

January 1991. Saddam Hussein's *Mother of all Battles* loomed. Chrys and Amanda flew back to London and into an uncertain world of shifting sands, of military misadventures, of qualified good, and of extended evil. Operation Desert Shield became Operation Desert Storm. It was all happening hundreds of miles away in the Arabian Desert, but everyone inside Flight 074 was gripped with fear and frustration as Trevor MacDonald recapped ITN News at 10 as piped in from the night of 15 January.

Touchdown, the passengers applauded the flight crew, relieved that what had gone through their minds didn't come to pass. Applause at landing, common on Nigeria Airways flights, came to British Airways on this day. Custom formalities over, Chrys and Amanda took the British Rail to Victoria. Vanessa was waiting.

Friday, January 18, Chrys came back to Southampton with Amanda. Too tired to go out, they retired early.

The next morning, Chrys fixed and served her breakfast in bed: beef sausages, smoked salmon, free-range omelette, decaffeinated tea, and the works. He turned on the television as she nibbled her toast. It was Gulf crisis galore. Day Four was a Saturday.

"....not another Vietnam; trust me, trust me," General Colin Luther Powell, the youngest ever Chairman of United States Chiefs of Joint Staff, lectured the media like a kinder, gentler headmaster on how to cut off Iraqi army and "kill it."

He flipped over to another channel. An armchair critic was talking philosophy. "War is raw. Forget the glamour of television. War is no fun; rather, it represents a remnant of man's bestiality, a trait that ties humanity to its descent from a barbaric tribe of brutes."

He flipped over to another channel. A group of experts was dissecting the war. One panellist was telling viewers how Mikhail Kalashnikov, a 28-year-old Red Army sergeant, invented *Avtomat Kalashnikova* in 1947, hence the name AK-47. A World War II veteran talked about the planning of D-Day half a century before and how it was won. A Falklands War hero said General Norman Schwarzkopf was going to be the greatest general since Douglas Macarthur. There was nothing else to watch. Chrys did not have cable or satellite service, so he turned off the television altogether and concentrated on his crunchy cornflakes.

The phone rang, as if waiting for the television to go off.

Adaora: "Happy New Year, traveller. How was it at home?"

"Great." Chrys gave her the details.

"Good. How's your book on dictators coming up?"

"I got more materials, salt-and-pepper stuff, but I've got to sort out my thesis."

"I told you no one would touch it, didnae I?" Adaora joked, imitating her Scottish mother-in-law. "So what's new?"

"As you know, your visit here had some side effects."

"She doesn't deserve you. With a name like an ass, I wouldn't take her back if she came back on all fours."

"Well, I found the angel reported missing from heaven." Amanda gave him a curious look, not sure what he was saying nor to whom.

"Anybody I know?" Adaora asked.

"Yes, she will be moving into your house next week."

"Amanda Arinze!"

"Don't sound too thrilled; there's no mark for guessing right."

"You smart son of a giddy gun! I told you about Mary and you went after her big sister. I don't remember telling you about her."

"No, you didn't." Chrys briefed her without revealing that Amanda was in his bed

"Which means you will be increasing my bills on weekends?"

"I am not complaining," Chrys chuckled.

At church the next day, Chrys saw Jackie walking up to receive Holy Communion. Before the service ended, she was gone. Chrys took Amanda over to Granby Grove to see Doreen Dearlove, Sean's girlfriend and Jackie's flatmate. She and Jackie had travelled to London. Monika, the German exchange student, offered them coffee.

Amanda left for London later that evening. The next Friday, he would travel up to London. She left without telling Chrys that she knew Jackie very well; he didn't tell her that he had just broken off with Jackie. It was a silly cover-up that seemed quite harmless at the time, except that the journey of a million miles starts with a single step.

****

Chrys had five days to unwind and to figure out the new turn in his life. He still found women of his era challenging, even complicated. He was more at home with mature ladies. Amaka, his real first love, was a single mother when he fell for her. In Igboland and for a high-school student his age, that took some nerve.

Gina Giacomelli was a manifestation of his wild teenage years in Europe. It was teenage lust for Latin

63

loveliness, nothing deep. Luckily, more mature and experienced Amaka was still available and clerking for his family business. His father dispatched her to Perugia to rescue the hapless youth. His dependence on the loyal and loving lady deepened, culminating in their flight from Italy with his daughter Kamemena.

Amaka was very mature, motherly, and fun. She was his mentor. Even after she had weaned him, he kept going back to her. She was more than a lover; she was a friend. His was an unadulterated juvenile lust for a real woman, an older woman without the complications of college chicks. He was not prepared to work hard at relationships. But Amaka now belonged to the past. He could not go back to her without risking a scandal that would sour everything because now Mrs. Amaka Arinze was about to become his stepmother-in-law.

In 1988 Britain, he met Jackie Onaga. She was academic about relationship, too clinical. They discussed every kiss, what was possible, what she would never do, and whose turn it was to watch the ceiling. Every little movement of the limbs was analysed. She seized the sizzle in the stew. She was predictable, no sense of adventure. To crown it, she was really bad in bed. Jackie admitted that she sometimes had her mind on Dolmio Lasagna. Chrys felt that the thought alone was crass; that she said it was cheap. He called her "Flat Domingo," which had both anatomical and musical connotations. Yet Chrys loved her. He loved challenges from women.

Amanda's unpredictability was intriguing and tickled him beyond belief. She was a tough act to follow, especially their most intimate moments. She loved Chrys. Many men had treated her as though she was there to be bought over with expensive gifts. As if that was not enough, no man had really cared about her intimate needs, something that nearly edged her over to the other side of sexuality with Sharon Innes, a co-worker at the

Citizens Advisory Bureau. Satisfied that it was not her, she decided to give normal relationship another go, after she must have ridden herself of the daddy-desertion disquiet that had wrecked her social life and encroached heavily on her otherwise straight sexuality. Chrys came along. She learned to love again, to relax, to laugh, and to cherish.

11

"I am supposed to produce a sensible rejoinder to an article before lunch tomorrow?" Chrys wondered aloud as he listened to the message left in his Ansaphone by the editor of *Wessex Weekly*. "I have not even read the piece."

****

An article had appeared on the everyday whipping horse: racism. Pete Alott, the paper's editor, knew Chrys's views on such issues and thought he was the person to put a hole to the claims of Daphne Peacock, who was running for the Union presidency. Many members of the editorial board of the free campus newspaper supported her. They were not only vocal about their support they shoved her down everybody's throat. They portrayed her as "Southampton Superwoman," the young socialist version of Margaret Thatcher. "Daph the Dyke," as she was known in gutter-press circles, was set to crush any opposition.

No matter how Pete tried to pilot meetings, the female-dominated editorial board stayed on his case. He considered the way they promoted Daphne undemocratic. Also, a good friend of his from the faculty of law was in the race. When Daphne sent in the article, Pete saw it as a ploy to appeal to the community of minority students because many of them were taking increasing interest in union affairs, thanks to Chrys's campaign. Though she meant well, it was definitely a vote-catching ploy, and he wanted equal time for other contestants.

****

Chrys knew all about Daphne's designs, but it was none of his business. Attacking Daphne, who was coming on as the champion of the oppressed, would be playing with a double-edged dagger. At best, he would be seen by both the minority and mainstream students as naive. On the other hand, he would be failing in his duty if he declined to comment.

"Hello love," Amanda's message came after Pete's. "Call me. Love you."

He dialled Adaora's London lair.

"Hello?" Amanda was waiting by the phone.

"What's up?" he inquired.

"I was wondering whether you could come up for the weekend."

"It is your turn, darling, remember?"

"I know. I just do not feel like another train ride down south. I will cook you something special. Please?" she pleaded.

Chrys decided to do an abstract draft and build it into Daphne's article. After supper, he read some materials from National Union of Overseas Students (NUOS) and looked up some quotations. Under "race," Sir Walter Raleigh (1861-1922) came up tops:

I wish I loved the Human Race;
I wish I loved its silly face;
I wish I liked the way it walks;
I wish I liked the way it talks;
I wish when I'm introduced to one
I wish I thought What Jolly Fun!

The man made more sense to Chrys than everything he had read that evening. He thought about his approach as he watched the BBC *9 O'clock News*. He would simply serve the words of Sir Raleigh and write on as if it just dropped in. When he finally switched on his Amstrad PC 1512 DD, the words flowed. He saved the document after running the spellchecker. He had a beer while he watched *American Top Ten* served by the local TVS. It was past midnight.

The telephone woke him up at about seven in the morning. Gina had just come in from a club and decided to talk to somebody.

"I feel really awful...." Gina informed in Italian.

"I know: plenty of booze and smoke-and-inhale stuff." There was no shred of sympathy in his voice. "Why don't you try and let the excess out?"

"I won't. You know I would be sick for weeks after that."

"That would keep you at home for awhile," he said with swarming sarcasm.

"Chrys, you are not being helpful."

"I'm sorry, signorita, but you must stop clubbing every night and stay off booze." He talked her into getting a cup of coffee and sleeping it off. He would call her at dawn, Toronto time.

Chrys could not go back to sleep. He got himself the same prescription and savoured the rich aroma. He cranked up his computer again, squeezed in a few of Daphne's words, and shortened the draft copy. Two hours later, he read the resultant four-page document:

"Daphne Peacock's 'Campus Racism' (*Wessex Weekly*, Xmas Edition) ruffled some feathers. The article is exciting and estimable. It is good to know that someone believes that our community is far from faultless. However, sincerely speaking, slogans do not address the hydra-headed issue of base bigotry."

It went on.

He erased an entire page that sounded more like a personal attack: Daphne was not "a patronising hypocrite." Pete would love it, but Chrys would not twist the knife. He adopted a constructive-criticism approach and rewrote the last page, adding that Daphne had the opportunity to champion the cause of overseas students at E & W. She failed.

Chrys left for London without calling Gina. He didn't forget; it just didn't seem very important. He had told her several times to cut down on drinking. He mumbled as he left the house, "If she wants to drown herself at the altar of Lord Bacchus, that's her funeral. No one tells the stubborn that a market stampede has ensued."

12

On his way to the station, Chrys dropped off the rejoinder at Pete's West Building office, on the north side of the campus. At Southampton Parkway, he parked his car and caught the 10.39 train to London Waterloo, a semi-fast schedule. He didn't mind. Every second without Amanda counted; she loved attention, and he obliged her.

Amanda was standing by the main WH Smith at Waterloo, opposite Platform 9. Chrys saw her immediately he walked out of Platform 10. She was wearing a pair of jeans and an overshirt, the tail of which was knotted for effective chic-and-cool look. She wore comfortable ankle boots with elasticised gussets. There was no mistaking her; there was nothing casual about her. Her hairdo and the gold-rimmed glasses always gave her an emphasised upmarket image,

"Hey, darling, what have we here?" Chrys admired the crew-neck, short-sleeved T-shirt with shouting rising-sun embroidery. She designed it.

"Why the Rising Sun, you were wondering?" she said smiling. He nodded. "Smashing, isn't it? I got the idea from a Biafran picture of my old man. You like?"

"Sure, it's terrific. I am a son of the Sun."

****

Colonel Chukwuemeka Arinze was prominent in the Republic of Biafra. He piloted the Biafran Bureau of State Security so well no coup plot saw the light of day. When breakaway Biafra broke, the boss of BOSS relocated to Côte d'Ivoire with the head of state, leaving his pregnant wife behind with three children. Sue Arinze, nee O'Brien, worked with the Caritas relief effort. Only the Sues of this world would marry Adnan Khashoggi and live in 1980s Beirut.

In Abidjan, Arinze fell for his secretary.

Sue found out about the secretary, who had effectively become his wife-in-exile, and that she was expecting his baby. After having the twins, Sue stayed back in Enugu for four years. The new Nigeria was too rich. She didn't lack anything. Arinze's father left enough wealth to dwarf the new oil-boom millionaires. But she didn't marry money; she married a man for love. Sue went back to Liverpool. Her parents were moving back to Ireland. She took over their house and stayed back to reactivate her Biafra-addled brain.

The family reunited in the O'Brien's retirement home in Killaloe-on-Shannon, County Clare, Ireland. Arinze started visiting as soon as the British government could allow it without stepping on the toes of General Gowon's Lagos regime. He agreed to leave the ex-secretary. Sue gave in. A year later, she found out the woman was living in Wimbledon, in same house where Sue had met him.

Sue knew the man she had married. Women were all over him the day she met him in the summer of 1960— the year of Nigeria's political independence from Britain. It was at the birthday party of his fiancée, a fellow Igbo-Nigerian named Virginia Obiageli Nebo. A fellow student at Hull, with whom Sue had a platonic relationship, had taken her to the party. She saw Emeka Arinze. He was at Oxford; he was loaded; and he was handsome. They clicked. Sue went back to Hull in his Rolls Royce. Obiageli vanished from the scene after she fled to Cardiff to complain to Arinze's cousin Cletus, who eventually married her.

When the Nigerian government pardoned all ex-Biafran officials, bar the ex-leader, Arinze flew back to Nigeria and set up Sanctus Securitas, an international security agency. Since Sue was done with Nigeria, and the ex-secretary lover loved London more, he married their wartime housemaid, pretty Perpetua Amaka Dike, who already had a son by him. Arinze and Sue remained friends. A devout Catholic, divorce was out of the question.

****

Amanda was so happy to see Chrys she could hardly concentrate on her driving. The weekend traffic was light, but it was dangerous to drive around London without paying attention. Traffic lights apart, pedestrians strive to claim their rights. The way some of them looked, if drivers came close to the zebra, one would think driving a car had become anti-social.

"Take it easy."

"I know you don't trust my driving, but I'm afraid you have to sit this one out." She grinned and patted his knee. "Relax! I'm not taking you to Spanish butchers, even though they now use general anaesthesia. It's EEC law."

Chrys had observed that they were not going in the direction of Finsbury, where she stayed with Adaora. He didn't ask. He forced a smile and tried not to encourage her lovey-dovey larks. They crossed the Thames at Westminster Bridge. All the buildings and parks were familiar: Big Ben, Westminster Abbey, signs to the Victoria Station, Hyde Park Corner, etc. They passed the French Embassy in Knightsbridge and headed towards Kensington. She raced past Hyde Park and turned off Kensington High Street.

He was not conversant with central London, but he had an idea where they were. It was one of those posh areas one saw ladies with groomed little dogs. The genetically engineered pets wore designer suits, had dental checkups, had their own fur dressers, and cost a bomb to keep.

Amanda parked in the street, a stone-throw from Holland Park, and invited him to follow her. Chrys complied.

They walked in through a small door, small because of the magnificent hallway that greeted them. He looked around as if he had seen such a place only on the pages of magazines. "Is this your old man's place?"

"Yes, and we are the new occupants. Smashing, huh? It won't be for long, just until you round up your programme and we move back home. In case you were wondering, he is not losing a penny. The Ivorian diplomat for whom it was rented decided Paris has all it takes. You know our Francophone brethren: fish out of water in London."

"Why don't you move down to Southampton?" Chrys requested.

"Not on your life! I don't want to hear myself think. No, you move up here and we can drive down once or twice a week to see your supervisor. We can spend a night at a bed-and-breakfast, if need be. I am not moving down to Hampshire to live in a bed-sit. Why the hassles when we have a place like this rent-free?"

"I guess you are right, but I'll have to think about it. Where is the kitchen? I'm starving."

"Sorry, love, but we have to drive down to Finsbury. The magic I promised is at Adaora's."

"Let's go then; I'm starving," he repeated.

"Not so fast, honey, you haven't seen the bedroom."

"After you," Chrys said with grim resignation.

They went upstairs. It was tastefully furnished. The master bedroom was adorned with a four-poster bed. Every mod-com was in immaculate condition. He was not one to be impressed by the rich-and-famous à la Hollywood décor. His tastes were simpler, but he was impressed. He had not been to that room, but he had been to the house. He was tempted to tell her, but he had already denied knowing it was her father's property.

"We are going to like it here," Amanda announced.

Chrys walked to the window and looked out. Birds flew in and out from Holland Park. Very few people walked up or down the street. He walked over to the entertainment centre. The CD collections reflected mature taste, nothing anybody would hear in *Top of the Pops*. He selected a Nat King Cole classic collection and keyed in a number.

"Unforgettable...." The soul-stirring velvet voice of the maestro Nat King Cole filled the air.

Chrys felt the warmth of human hand round his neck. He turned round and saw Amanda wearing a bathrobe with her initials "AA" blazoned on the mock breast pocket. She gave him one. It was green; hers was pink. He took it, unfolded it, and saw his initials: "CC."

"Thanks," he said. "That was very thoughtful of you. Oh, if the last 'A' is for Arinze, then it has to change to 'C' soon."

"If you ask me nicely, deal. Now put it on and let's see the bathroom."

"Thank you, I have had a shower."

"I know. I am not asking you; I am telling you."

He left his trousers and shirt on the dressing stool. On a second thought he took it to the large wardrobe. It was full with items of clothing.

"Hey, who owns this boutique, some cocaine baron?"

"Government stock; you can help yourself later. Come on," she urged.

He followed her into the bath, which turned out to be a Jacuzzi with collapsible transparent roof. He looked up. Planes queued up to land at Heathrow; they popped out of the smoggy sky at almost regular intervals. She was already in the water blocking its spiral pump-propelled flow. Soon, rich leather foam formed and gave out a very pleasant smell of organic passion-fruit essence. He did not believe in aphrodisiacs, and she knew he had no need for one. Besides, common wisdom has it that no one spits out honey.

13

As they left the bedroom, Chrys said, "It is a screaming shame to sacrifice such smooth comfort for a passion-fruit bath."

"I don't mind if we square the score," Amanda offered.

"The square of one is not two. In any case, you would have to tie my hands and gag me."

"Oh no, I'm not into bondage and kinky stuff."

"Please take me to some place I can smell F-O-O-D; I am into that."

"Old man!"

Amanda piloted her father's sleek Sierra Sapphire across the City of London and headed towards Pentonville Road. At Finsbury, they ate and had an agreeable evening chatting and drinking with Adaora. The okra soup with pounded yam was the magic Amanda had promised. Chrys knew she didn't cook it; she had not been exposed to the magic of Igbo culinary art. She did help Adaora though, judging by the way she explained the cooking formula. He gave her all the credits, winking at Adaora when she wasn't looking.

"If you do that again, I'll tell her," Adaora rebuked him when Amanda went to get something from the kitchen.

"Just try it and I'll say you told me," Chrys threatened.

Chrys had a tête-à-tête with Adaora before they left Finsbury. He lost the argument about not wanting to move up to London. He hated big cities, be it Lagos, Rome, or New York. For this reason he refused to go to Kings College, Lagos and turned down admission to the

University of Rome. He went on to Rutgers, New Brunswick for his graduate degree, instead of Columbia University, New York.

"You can call it 'acute metrophobia.' If my supervisor had invited me to join him at the University of London, I would have passed. Believe me, I don't like big cities. I feel like I am being suffocated. Marriage is not going to change that."

"Marriage? You are not married," Adaora reminded him.

"The marital rites have reached advanced stages. How much is the dowry at Ndinze, eh? Two thousand naira, that's one hundred pounds at most."

"Don't be a prat. Chief Arinze does not need your bleeding money. You haven't got a penny to your name.... Ph.D. does not mean pounds, shillings, and pence. Her grandpa's money sustains a bank in England."

"Wait a sec, Adaora. What I meant to say was that we are, according to our customary law, married. It has absolutely nothing to do with money. You don't buy people. Dowries are meant to seal an agreement, not convey currency assessment."

"Okay, I guess I was looking at it purely from...."

"London point of view? You see why some of you should move out of this urban jungle of concrete-steel carbuncle at least once every other year. The traditional ceremony will eventually be the rock upon which the marriage survives. Without it, all the until-death-do-us-part and for-richer-for-poorer farce out here don' mean a thing."

"Doesn't, Mr. M. A. Americana!"

"Whatever."

"Just do the right thing," Adaora admonished.

"What do you mean?" Chrys asked.

"Take her to the Registry; forget about your mother's chronic Catholicism."

Chrys was surprised. "Did Adaeze say that?"

"No, but why would she take the house off the market for the year?"

"She said...."

"I know what she said. Extra money wouldn't hurt Chief Arinze, even if he were the Sultan of Brunei."

Chrys proposed all over again.

Amanda was expecting it. She accepted. She would buy the ring of her choice that week.

Chrys walked into marriage with eyes wide open. It was not on his agenda. He found the corridors of academia a place to hide. The ivory tower harboured all sorts. It was a place one could be both irresponsible and insensitive and still got away with it. Campuses have hotheads, political agitators, Nobel laureates, professors, paedophiles, etc. He wouldn't want to grow old without some decorum, but he was not ready to serve just one daughter of Eve.

On Sunday, they went over to Ossie's place in Plaistow. Ossie worked in the marketing division of a multinational company. His father was the younger brother of Chrys's father; his mother, the elder sister of Jackie's mother. From there, they drove to North London to see Aunt Pat. Seamus elected to give her away. Pat and Seamus had two boys; Amanda was the daughter she always wanted. She had mothered and pampered her whenever she came over on holidays. When she became pregnant, Pat stayed with her in Killaloe until she gave birth to Amina. After her undergraduate studies at Ahmadu Bello University, Zaria, Nigeria, Amanda came back to England for her masters. She stayed with the Kellys. Seamus was no stranger to the Arinzes. Colonel Arinze saved his life in 1968, while he reported the

Nigeria-Biafra War for a London broadsheet. It was Sue's letter to Pat that got them together.

Amanda and Chrys drove back to West London. They watched some television. Gulf War was still on every channel. Some expert was saying that the ecological warfare launched from Al Wafra oilfields, termed "environmental terrorism" by the Pentagon, would accelerate Allied response. The fact that US Defence Secretary Dick Cheney and General Colin Powell visited the area supported his analysis, he claimed.

It was now about 9 PM. Chrys had to leave. Amanda objected. His worst fear had just begun: He had lost a large lump of his liberty.

14

Chrys could not convince Amanda easily that he must go back to Southampton. He knew then that his fear of marriage was well-grounded. The scheduled Monday morning meeting with Professor Alan Prichard, his supervisor, was crucial to an upcoming seminar and to his viva, and it might be another month before Alan returned to Britain. Inviting Chrys to join him for the three-year study of the European Economic Community was in recognition of his research capability, which Alan had noted at Rutgers. Chrys registered for a postgraduate degree in political science. In the 1989/90 Awards Scheme, he got the Overseas Research Students (ORS) award, which subsidized his tuition. Alan paid a monthly stipend, and Chrys taught his classes.

Amanda caved in reluctantly after extracting a promise that he would come up again by Friday. Chrys caught the past-midnight train, which didn't stop at Parkway. He took a taxi from Central station back to Parkway to pick up the car before clamp-happy ticket controllers noticed.

He played back the Ansaphone as soon as he crept into his room. "Hi, it's me again. Pete. Thanks for the article. I was just wondering if you could change the last page. Continue on the theme of offensive... patronising hypocrisy. I'll pick it up tomorrow from your office, or you can email it to me. Thank you."

"You did promise to call. You are a bad man, Chrys." Gina sounded her old self.

Back in his office after meeting with Alan, Chrys saw the article Pete has returned. He read aloud the last sentence. "Role models are good and great, as long as you do not fight designer discrimination with deliberate discrimination, positive or negative. Two wrongs don't make a right." With his left hand, he dropped the article in the wastepaper basket.

Chrys was on his way out when the phone rang. Pete said he would pick up the article later that evening. "You are very welcome. It will be where you had left it. Feel free to make changes, but do not append my name to any alteration whatsoever that is not grammatical, libellous, or politically incorrect."

Chrys drove to Bordon in the southeast of Hampshire to visit a family. Pete came to pick up the article, but he could not locate it. Since he was running late for class, he took a fat folder on the table, hoping the article would be inside it.

Back to base, Chrys returned Amanda's many calls. She told him what she had been up to; he, about his trip.

"Have you told your countrywoman?" she inquired.

"Who?"

"Jackie," she giggled. "Any way, I've beaten you to it. She wishes us all the best. I had called Doreen, and she… Jackie answered the phone. She would have heard it from Dor anyway. Feel free to invite her."

Chrys stayed home and made corrections along the lines Alan had suggested. After the BBC news at 9 PM, Jackie called.

"I hear you've heard," Chrys said in Igbo.

"So, you sent your *yeye* woman to do your dirty job?"

"Hey, don't be rude. She thought I had told you."

"She should have waited for me to congratulate her! 'Have you heard the wonderful news?' It was as if Christ came back."

"That doesn't make her a *stupid* woman."

"Tell that to your *yeye* woman!" she cursed. Before she banged the phone, she added, "Tell her that a drunken fowl has not met a mad fox."

It was Thursday before Chrys went up to the campus. He was at the Union shop to pick up a packet of cigarettes.

"Excuse me, Chrys, may I have a word," Daphne demanded. "What is this article I heard you have written attacking me?"

"It's a rejoinder to yours; my personal perspective, that is."

"That's not what I saw," Daphne protested.

"Correction: *heard*; I have not submitted the article."

Lunch break, Pete came to the office.

"I got your email. I am sorry about the misinformation. I had misplaced the article. What work were you on about?"

"The one about dark dictators; is it part of your thesis?"

"Oh no, it's a book I am writing," Chrys informed him.

"Have you tried publishing it?"

"Do I have blood in my veins? The only hope is vanity."

"As long as you part with a substantial sum from your building-society account?"

"That's the general idea. Problem is, Pete, I do not have a building-society account."

"Do you still intend to publish it?" Pete was not joking.

"Sure. It may not be a bestseller, but I intended to share it. Now that you have skimmed through, I've scored."

"Chrys, I didn't *skim*; I read it twice."

"Why would you do that to yourself!"

"I like it, and I will publish it," Pete declared matter-of-factly.

"It's all yours!"

"I am serious, Chrys. Seventy-thirty, if you don't mind."

"Mind?" They shook hands on it. One would expect Chrys to be over the moon, but he wore a cynical smile that didn't mask his doubt. "Now that we have got that out of the way, who told Daph about my piece?"

"Oh, they have reached her? Anyway, I'm no longer interested in Daphne and her cohorts of man-hating Amazons on the editorial board. I have to think of life after here."

"This reminds me, I am wedding sometime next month or so."

"Congratulations! You know, I saw her over the weekend. She really looked like she's been doing a lot of running around."

"Who?" Chrys was surprised.

"The lawyer. It's her… she is not?"

"Jackie and I broke up late last year, thanks to the Union."

"That's why you resigned?"

"Yes, but that's one scoop you won't repeat in *Wessex Weekly*."

"Now you see why I want to quit," Pete said triumphantly.

"What about your friend?"

"My chairmanship of the editorial board isn't going to help him much. There are rules. Daphne is now monitoring every little print. The sexist card is now hollow, since she is not the only female in the race. I do not want any of her argy bargy. I'll still do my best for my friend, but the whole thing has been polarised by partisan party politics."

Thursday, 28 February 1991, the Gulf War ended. The hot weather would have set in by March, and the holy month of Ramadan was to begin on March 17. The Union elections were held as and when due. Daphne lost the Labour rose-banner, badly bloodied by militant leftists. The Tory torch-bearer, Pete's friend, also lost. His gospels came unadulterated from the books of hardcore Thatcherism. The Lib-Dem bird, a true lark, had one item on her manifesto: proportional representation. Armed with the Original Plant Report (of Professor Raymond Plant and later Labour's Lord Plant of Highfield), she convinced few. The Green guy talked about socio-environmental consciousness, about saving heavens because "our earth is already dead," and about "the wonderful Stone Age."

An engineering student of unknown political pigmentation won. Rumours of rigging were rife, but the returning officer said he had nothing to hide. "There was no jiggery-pokery," he said, "no hidden agenda." He sounded very convincing, but heading the victory parade for the new kiddo on the block was not exactly what many people saw as a show of neutrality.

It was the end of an era. Chrys bade bye-bye to campus politics because the ocean never swallows a person with whose leg it does not come in contact.

15

The council celebrant had problems with the names at the rehearsal. He believed that pronouncing names wrongly during such an important, video-recorded occasion should be avoided.

"I'm sure the man will still get the names wrong," Amanda said as Chrys parked the car in front of Ossie's house.

"It don' matter," Chrys said with a New Jersey dismissive demeanour.

"It does," she shot back.

****

It mattered to Amanda. Her parents never meant to call her "Amanda." She was to be named after Arinze's aunt and baptized "Mary" after Sue's aunt, who was a renowned reverend sister. Her father was at Cambridge doing his masters; her mother, who had graduated from Hull, was visiting her folks in Liverpool. Contractions came, and she went into labour. The midwife requested for a name. Weak and still trying to get over the first experience, Sue handed her a note. It read "*ADANMA*," which is Igbo and in which *ada mma* means "beautiful daughter." The Merseyside maternity matron felt it was wrongly spelt and *corrected* it to "AMANDA." Before anybody realised it, it had entered into official records. Disappointed but happy, Emeka Arinze squeezed in an "A" to remind him of the name that wasn't to be.

The "A" didn't stand for anything; there was no way his daughter was going to bear two similar names, one being an anagram of the other. Calling her "Amina" after his mother was deemed dodgy. It was complicated enough that the baby girl had parents from different cultural backgrounds, compounding her Christianity with Islam was not a prospect Arinze cherished.

When his father passed on in 1966, Emeka Arinze took the family to Enugu for the state funeral. Sue was pregnant with Loretta. The Nigeria-Biafra War grounded them in Nigeria. Everyone called Amanda "Adaeze," probably because her great grandfather was Eze of Ndinze. After the war, she still preferred the name, but it never really stuck because schools recognized only names on paper and local Catholic Church clergies had not embraced the use of African names.

****

Ossie's house was full of friends taking up assignments. Amanda's friend and ex-colleague Sharon Innes was waiting. They went upstairs to look at her antique wedding gown, taking with them two cups of Dublin coffee.

"Having a second thought?" Sharon asked Amanda.

"I don't know. Months ago, I was asserting my independence. Today, all I want is a man and loads of lovely kids."

"Like all good Catholic girls!"

"Sharon, I don't know if I am doing the right thing by Amina, and there is an Italian tigress to tame... not his daughter; no, Kameme is an absolute angel. Chrys and his ex bring out the worst in humanity."

"Come on, love, Chrys is a nice bloke. You don't find many like him these days. Intelligent, handsome... great sense of humour, caring, and he is not gay."

"Hey, hey, hold it there! Is he paying you?"

The wedding was well-attended. Ossie was the best man; Sharon, the chief bridesmaid. Amanda rolled out her father's now-vintage Rolls Royce. Jackie did not attend the wedding. Doreen came with Sean; Pete, with a girlfriend.

The newlyweds left for their honeymoon, a secret destination known only to the donors, Mr. and Mrs. Kelly. On the A4 to Heathrow, they opened the envelope. Venice was wonderfully welcoming that spring. They checked into their hotel, freshened up, and joined the sea of tourists.

They strolled leisurely on Piazza San Marco and went into the magnificent Basilica for holy water, signs of the cross, and silent prayers. They walked along the narrow cobbled lanes and stopped at one of the restaurants. Amanda was enjoying herself at a nightclub, but Chrys stretched his Italian to ridiculous limits. She was almost cut off the moment a group of teeny-weeny wannabes joined their table. Belated translations were punctuated with more Italian, which had to be translated. Chrys was so plastered with wines he passed out on the couch the moment they returned to their room.

The next day, Chrys was back to his romantic self: flowers, attention, and sweet talks. Amanda was impressed, but she made it clear his Italian made her look dumb. He apologised and promised to make it up to her. He did not speak any Italian all day long, which was good because the gondola-serenade ride was translation-free. That night, Chrys made up for the previous night. They woke up, ate, slept… punctuated only by whatever came naturally in-between.

Two weeks later, armed with Venetian crafts and gifts, they left behind the irresistible and magical delights of *Bride of the Sea* and headed back west. Italy brought back memories, especially the seventh stopover at the Shrine of St. Chrysogonus. Amanda was sleeping soundly; Chrys watched her. Events had moved so fast he hadn't had the time to take stock. One good thing was that everyone in his family accepted Amanda without reservations; her family, him. Gina wouldn't have had such a passage. Amanda was not only considered local she was almost family.

"Has Amanda some Sue in her?" Chrys wondered. To expect her to posses the virtues of Mary O'Brien and Sue Arinze would be asking for a crate of coloured clouds or, as they said in Kene community, a gallon of grasshopper's urine. There was some Sue in her genes, but there was more of the Arinze arrogance and the ability to make the impossible plausible; the seemingly impossible, possible. Chrys was in many ways a 1990s Arinze without the money to burn. As with most male species, the urge to roam about or the primitive wanderlust was very strong in him. He needed challenges to keep him sane because, as the proverbial ground squirrel has it, he who walks should sometimes break into a trot, in case the need to run arises. He was determined to give marriage his best shot, but the Chryses of this world are everyday men: flesh, bone, and blood. And there was a girl called Jackie O.

16

Sir Andrew Alott was a 20-year member of parliament for a Shire county constituency and a minister of the Crown, until he parted ways with the Iron Lady in 1982 "to spend more time with his family." The son of a Czech-Jew immigrant, he had married the only daughter of a Little London publisher, Sir Peter Bolus, who bequeathed everything to his daughter, Anne. A knight, captain of industry, and established publisher, Sir Drew, as he was affectionately called by constituents and colleagues, became a respectable backbencher in the House of Commons and a prominent member of the 1892 Committee.

Pete was the only son. He came to Southampton with an eye on maritime law. He lost interest in the course and changed to political science. And his path and Chrys's crossed.

****

Chrys and Amanda arrived at Bolus headquarters on the outskirts of Oxford. Pete's car was parked in front of the office. "PUKEMARK" was written on a trendy metal board in gold over a black background. The emblem was the head of a Queen's guardsman throwing up.

"Welcome to my world," Pete said as they were ushered into his large office. "I am glad to see you again, ma'am. This man here is supposed to be my business partner, but he chose to be a sleeping partner. In his position, I would do exactly the same!"

"Pee, sarcasm will not get you anywhere."

"Chrys, please allow the lady to acknowledge my compliments."

"Thank you, Pete," Amanda said with all the femininity in her. "I'm afraid I have to leave you two to it. I'll be back in an hour... two."

Chrys walked her to the car.

The two men talked about Southampton and the forthcoming graduation ceremonies before settling down to review the returned reviews. Some questions were raised by a political commentator Sir Drew had recommended. The man virtually rewrote a section of the book. Red ink was everywhere: passages to be eliminated, sentences to be rephrased, names to exclude, and possible libels here and there.

"The commentator believes there's democracy in Kenya."

"The piece has got absolutely nothing to do with that brand of democracy. When you preclude others from exercising their right to vote and be voted for, that is not democracy."

"Okay, he also reckons that the burning of elephant tusks by President Daniel arap Moi was not an economic blunder but a fine political point, an ecological and economic commonsense."

"I don't know the colour of the man's politics, Pee, but burning those ivories was an ecological and economic disaster. Every kindergarten kid knows."

Pete approved. "The siSwati son of King Sobhuza II, ex-Sherborne soccer star, monarch Mac of Mbabane... MAKAHO... 67th son?!"

"Makhosetive Dlamini, King Mswati III of Swaziland; stinking rich, six wives, and more beautiful virgins are to come with each anniversary."

"And he's not yet 24? My dear Chrys, you guys have characters down there."

"Don't you start!"

"*Pardon moi*; it's your work."

"Keep your comments to yourself until you've bought a copy!"

Pete laughed as he flipped over a few more pages and then back. The commentator appeared to have concentrated on Kenya. He went for a dog-eared page somewhere in the middle. "Samuel Doe, isn't he a general like others?"

"Wasn't," Chrys corrected. "I prefer the rank he earned: master sergeant. Insert 'later promoted himself General, Life President, and Commander-in-Chief.'"

Pete made a note of it and continued, "The description of his death is gruesome."

"Wacky, isn't it? I saw a pirated copy of the video. You wouldn't want to watch it. Whoever recorded it must have his bowels examined; it churned mine just watching it."

"I hope it doesn't get us into trouble."

"Pee, the man is dead."

"Foreign Office might not like us to paint the perpetrators as potheads."

"Bullocks! My country lost men and money keeping Charles Taylor at bay so Doe could make hay. Oh no, there's nothing as reliable as the equatorial sun. But it sets. It set on Doe. Anyway, let us not speak ill of the departed; it's un-African."

"Ivory Coast."

"Felix Houphouët-Boigny of Côte d'Ivoire is 86. The Basilica of Our Lady of Peace in Yamoussoukro, his birthplace, is a wonder of the century. It was kept a shade lower than St Peter's Basilica as a mark of respect to the Vatican."

"You don't seem to condemn it?"

"Mr. Publisher, haven't you noticed that I do not judge? I present facts known and published."

"Field Marshal Idi Amin. Dada? I like the encounter with Gentleman Jim Callaghan in the Hills Affair. You make the guy look like a gentle giant."

"He became a megalomaniac after the Asians had gone. You see, when what you perceive as the source of your worries is removed and your worries won't go away, you look elsewhere. Fear rolls in its army of hate, and whoever is not for you is against you."

"Could we dwell more on Jim's visit and remove the ridiculous order to print more money as a means of tackling inflation?"

"Pee, please do not lose sight of the working title. It's not an unauthorised biography of the last Labour PM this century, probably."

"I'll second that," Pete said with a smirk.

"I guess the others are pretty in order. Oh, I need more beef on General Gowon, who said that money was not the problem but how to spend it."

"I included his use of hunger as a weapon of war and his pathetic postwar policies. We have had wackier politicians in Nigeria, so let's not flog it."

"No wonder you want them back in diplomatic crates."

Chrys ignored the remark.

Pete continued, "Over to the Caribbean Islanders. The Duvalier Dynasty—Francois 'Papa Doc' Duvalier and 'Baby Doc' Jean-Claude—is pretty in order. These Indian-Ocean islands are out of the way. I am more worried about the spellings of names."

"It doesn't matter. Libyan leader Gadaffi has defied spellcheckers and he is nearer to your centre of civilisation."

A secretary wheeled in a trolley of steaming pots and snacks.

"*Merci*, Marie," Pete said. She beamed a warm continental smile and promptly made her exit. Pete picked up the telephone, which Chrys did not hear ring. "Show her in." He stood up and straightened his tie. "Welcome, Ma'am."

"Am I intruding?"

"No, you got here right on time. Look, we are about to have tea," Pete said, feeling unnecessarily uncomfortable in his suffocating politeness.

"Hello, darling," Chrys said "I hope you didn't buy Oxford!"

The sandwiches were delicious, and the tea was great.

When they rose to leave, Pete invited them to Sir Drew's nearby country estate. "Mandy must meet my Mom, Lady Anne," he said. Chrys looked at Amanda. She shrugged. "Good, let's go. Hey, please don't forget to tell her how good the garden looks."

"Praise her biscuits, don't drop the tea cup, don't forget it is 'Milady,' and agree with everything she says," Chrys interjected, but Amanda did not find his comments funny. She knew Chrys would step over bounds if encouraged because a dancing madman does not require an orchestra.

Chrys and Amanda drove back to London. They were happy with the trip, but Amanda found Pete's enthusiasm a bit over the top.

17

Chrys was at Gatwick Airport to see Amanda off in June 1991. She was going to Lagos to pick up Kamemena. They wanted her to get to know Amina. They clung to each other until the last call.

"Don't do anything I won't do, honey," she said.

"Deal, darling," Chrys replied.

She walked on without looking back. It was her way of coping with the separation. He went over to the public viewing gallery and waited for the plane to take off. He remembered the unforgettable moments they had had inside the same flight just months before. Not even in dreams did he ever imagine such things coming his way within a short space and time.

On the Gatwick Express back to Victoria, Chrys reflected on his feelings for Amanda. She was a tigress when he met her. She had become a dear. She merely existed the year before; now she was living. He fished out his pocket notebook and started a poem that eventually shaped and ended thusly:

My thoughts raced back to things left undone,

Things said, things desired, and things done.

Off went the harbinger of anxiety into the atmosphere,

Polluting with toxic and noisy emissions the biosphere.

Noisily but successfully it left with my woman,

Leaving alone at the Airport a lonely man.

Back in London, he completed the poem, rearranged it, and addressed it to Amanda. He was about to leave the next morning when Sharon phoned. She wanted to drop Amanda's bound graduate thesis titled "*The Farce of Secularism in Nigeria.*"

"Come in, stay as long as you want. I wanted to leave because it's empty without her."

"I know the feeling."

"No, you don't; you are a woman."

"How very observant, sir!"

"What will it be?"

"The usual," Sharon said with a glee. "Go easy on whisky, if it's English."

"Neither shaken nor stirred?" Chrys asked knowingly. She gave him a thumb up. *The usual* was BMW—Baileys, Malibu, and Whisky.

The short visit rolled into late evening. Chrys locked up and drove her home, seven no-ice BMWs later. He turned into Southampton Way in Peckham and drove onto Rotherhithe Tunnel via Jamaica Road. He was in Plaistow just as Vanessa was coming back from evening church service with their children.

Early in July 1991, the book went to bed. Pete gave it his all. He called Chrys constantly to clear up a few problems. Chrys decided to drive up to the Oxford. He phoned Jackie and asked her along.

"Hey, no strings attached; you'll have a good time."

"You would say that, wouldn't you? If you must go with a woman, try Derby Road."

"I've got taste." Chrys knew Jackie was still bitter, but he wanted them to remain friends. "Call me if you change your mind."

He drove into the premises and parked besides Pete's car, his Grandpa's Austin-Harley. Pete was using every facility Bolus had, yet publishing the book was proving an uphill task. He turned out to be a perfectionist. Even after everything was thought to be okay, he still came up with questions for Chrys.

"I just got a late return from a commentator; it's about *Ngwazi*... the Conqueror Hastings Kamuzu Banda. He's worried about the Israeli-trained Young Pioneers. They don't terrorise citizens who disagree with the government, do they?"

"They are licensed to promote the extremities of the Malawi Congress Party, the only party in the country. How they go about it, I don't know. Surely, the commentator is not saying that building an 'Eton in the bush' is a white elephant?"

"No. In fact, he commended it. Others would prefer Mercedes limousines and personal palaces in Europe."

"Not to mention funds siphoned off to Swiss accounts."

Chrys drove back the way he came. Southbound traffic was light. He selected an FM radio station, but some other station preferred that band. He pushed in a cassette tape. The sanitized reggae of UB 40 filtered out of the speakers. It soon got to the turn of Cher-Sonny Bono hit song. He sang along, *"I got you babe... I got you babe...."*

18

The book was in the market within weeks. Vanessa organised a book launch at her church. It was well-attended, but the guests were mostly out to party than to contribute to literary art. Chrys knew it was a waste of time trying to get people to read books that were not about sex, scandal, soap gossip, and more sex.

Sunday after the Saturday event, Chrys was sleeping upstairs at Ossie's Plaistow pad. "Chiké, pick up the phone," Vanessa shouted from the lounge. "It's Pete."

"Hello, Mr. Maxwell Macmillan," Chrys joked.

"How did it go?"

"Cool. Nothing extraordinary, but the word has gone forth."

"Good. Can we meet tomorrow and discuss future logistics?" Pete requested.

"Sure."

"I need you to prepare for some talk shows. *This Morning Show* couple will bite, if anyone cancels midweek. I've phoned Oprah's people. They will get back to me."

"Go easy, boy; Oprah does not do political books."

"Chrys, it's a gamble."

They met at a restaurant in Waterloo at ten o'clock the next day. Pete was a bit late. He was delayed by the manager of a bookshop in Camberwell. He was creating new markets and outlets because smaller outlets took less commission. He wanted Chrys to come up on Friday and arrange with the manager for an autograph party.

"I promised to sign, not seal signing-session deals," Chrys asserted. The waiter brought their order. He waited for her to leave. "Pete, I have made it clear that my work comes first. What else do you want? Blood?"

"Blood, no; sweat, yes. Thereafter, you can retire to your Highfield hibernating house for middle-aged monks."

Chrys smiled and said, "At this rate, give me a middle-aged monk any day."

"Chrys, we are talking strategies, promotional logistics designed to work. At least come in for the signing session."

"How can I when it hasn't been okayed?" Chrys sounded irritated.

"How could I when I don't know if you are coming or going?"

"Okay, I'll ask somebody to help. Sean."

"Sean Kelly?"

"Yes, my woman's cousin. He can do with some exposure."

"What is he supposed to do?" Pete asked cynically. "Answer to your name or what?"

"That's an idea. A week stay at the Riviera and a few people would be fooled by his tan."

"Ha! Ha! Ha! That's funny!"

"Pee, I am serious. He can do the running around as my agent for twenty percent of my cut and commission on books he sells. If I must do any book signing, I won't have to appear first for preliminary interviews with managers of roadside bookshops."

Sean was thrilled. He went to work. Doubting Pete could not believe his luck when Sean secured a fill-in slot in a *Radio One* programme for first-time novelists. Chrys was not a novelist; he wrote a historical book. Pete called Chrys on the day of the interview.

"Pete dear, I can't make it to London in one hour and half. It's practically impossible, even if you send Superman."

Chrys tuned in and listened from his campus office. Poor Pete, he tried to talk his way through a book with names he couldn't remember, names he hardly knew how to pronounce, and places he could not point out in an atlas the size of a modest room. The host had not heard of the book until Pete gave him one.

"Yes, it is quite a comprehensive casebook, very enlightening and entertaining." Pete was obviously reading a prepared text.

"How is the book doing so far?" the host asked.

"As a first-time publisher publishing a first-time writer, it is early days yet and…."

"It won't be until the end of the week before we know if it has made it to the best ten in Britain," the host interrupted with unmasked cynicism.

It was all commerce and little on substance. Then again, if people knew the substance, they might not buy the book.

That evening, a flat *Soundbyte Show* gave Sean an idea. He phoned Chrys and asked if he would be interested in doing the show. Chrys gave him the go-ahead. Sean secured a slot. His father knew the producer of the show.

Sean called Chrys again midweek. "The deal is done," he announced as if he had a Saddam-signed piece of paper granting the Kurds political independence.

Cowboy publishing appeared to have triumphed.

19

Chrys appeared for the seven-minute interview. Only his introduction, the interpretation of the full name of Zairian President (Joseph Desire) Mobutu Sese Seko, and the hyped remarks by the host drew applause from the youthful audience. Chrys had read somewhere that Mobutu Sese Seko Kuku Ngbendu Waza Banga translated as "the cock that leaves no hen unconquered." He knew it wasn't so and, since the main aim of his book was to enlighten and entertain, he used the forum to put that right. He had lifted the meaning from *The Guardian* as "the all-powerful warrior who, because of his endurance and inflexible will to win, will go from conquest to conquest leaving fire in his wake." How the English translation equated with the shorter name, nobody asked. Chrys didn't know either.

The fast-talking host concluded, "And until next week, when we will have the man the media hate to love, the talk of the Big Apple, this is your host Josh Wosh on the super *Soundbyte Show* saying, sleep soundly but keep an eye here!"

One week after the show, the book went nowhere near the top-thousand bestsellers. It looked as if only a divine intervention would stir anybody to part with a hard-earned tenner. The book was not selling. However, fate has a way of turning banality into history, villains into heroes, and unsung books into classics. Someone somewhere saw the book and alerted a hitherto unknown group of fundamentalist Rastafarians called "*Rastamuffins*." Their interest must have been aroused by the interview because it was suddenly *Soundbyte Show* left, right, and centre.

It started with a simple letter to the book publisher, signed by one "I Babylon," threatening Armageddon if the book was not withdrawn. Pete promptly publicised the threat. He called a press conference and denounced "all attempts to crush creative minds." The tabloid press picked it up in small filler columns. A week later, the Rastamuffins took to the streets of South London.

Chrys was watching the early evening news at 5.40. The newscaster was cued to go over live to an OB camera crew covering the demonstration. "Sally Ann, what are they on about?"

"Fiona, I can't tell you exactly. Someone I spoke with awhile ago said that… I quote, 'The insults heaped on Emperor Haile Selassie must not go unpunished in Jah Babylon.' Unquote."

"Did they say what they want?"

"Everything they say is coded in some lingo that is not very English, if you ask me. Some sing about war and rumours of war…. Oh, you can hear the song: 'Everywhere is war….' Wait a minute, a bystander has just been given us a copy of the book. It is titled *WASTED WEALTH: The Wacky World of Dark Dictators*. The author is named Chrys Chaike Chaime."

"What is the book about?"

"Stone me to death if I have a clue. Oh, look… they are burning several copies of the book down the road. Fiona, we have to back off from here for now. This is Sally Ann Chadwick in South London. Come on guys; let's move it!" She ran further down the road, creating the impression that it was turning into a riot.

"Thank you Sally Ann," Fiona Fairkettle said, looking bemused by the fuss about a book set ablaze on a wire string. She turned to the studio camera: "More on that in our later bulletin."

Chrys listened to the 6 O'clock news. The demo was mentioned but with none of the drama that Sally Ann served half an hour earlier.

More protests brought the book to national and international attention. It was like a dream Chrys had not dreamt, but it was happening. The Rastamuffins intensified their protests peacefully. They were ignored after a couple of days. However, when a down-and-out Peckham bookshop that allegedly stored the book went up in flames, the mainstream media took note.

The Scum, a sleazy tabloid, appeared to be getting all the exclusives. Its circulation soared, especially among the so-called minorities, leaving the other tabloids wondering how they blew it. It was revealed that the Rastamuffins were ordered by Chief Priest Jahlove Rastaman to keep the book out of circulation "by all necessary and possible means." The reverse was the result. The book received reviews that otherwise would have required the publicity superpower of Saatchi and Saatchi.

"I don't believe it either," Chrys said when Amanda phoned to touch base. "You must come back here, honey."

"That's another reason why I am calling. With all the demos and threats, I think you should come home instead for the summer. The autumn will send those yobbos back to their caves."

"Okay, I'll think about it. I promise."

The book went up and stayed up. Chrys stayed back for the summer. In Southampton and away from all the London razzmatazz, he went about undisturbed. Sean secured numerous interviews, but Chrys would not appear. He said it would not be wise to show his face at that point. A special appearance was sought by EX Channel, makers of the suddenly popular *Soundbyte Show*, but Chrys won't bite. Seamus eventually intervened and asked him to appear on a daytime television show.

"Glory who?" Chrys asked.

"Ms. Shantcross, the golden girl," Seamus informed. "She promised to be sensible about it; besides, it could help to cool things a bit. Some positive publicity at this time won't hurt. She is highly regarded."

Glory Shantcross was looking her best, striving to live up to the media-tag of "Oprah Winfrey of Europe." A Los Angeles-Olympics medallist, she was shaping *Shantcross Show* with all her might and pulling every string her hands could reach. Built along the lines of Danish damsel Brigitte Nielsen, but with a redistributed and nature-balanced boob-and-butt build, there were not many macho strings she shouldn't be able to pull.

The interview proper started with a general review of Chrys's curriculum vitae: where he came from; what he was doing in the UK; what gave him the idea for the book; who sponsored the travels; what-have-you and what-have-you-not. The rapport established, Glory moved over to the "funny aspects of the book."

Chrys interjected, "The story of Bokassa and his two Vietnamese 'daughters' is not funny. It is a human tragedy. It is a story of how one man can ruin the lives of many."

She continued, "There were women from everywhere in his imperial life. Was the Romanian wife actually a personal present from Europe's last Stalinist, Comrade Nicolae Ceauşescu?"

"I don't know. Then again the Communist bureaucracy approved any marriage between a citizen and a foreigner, be he or she from Alaska or Australia,

Belgium or Burma; be it between tennis superstars Bjorn Borg and Simona Simonescu, or between Ilie Iliescu and say… Samantha Socks from Sussex."

The audience laughed and applauded.

"Moving up north towards the 'Queendom of Sheba,' you picked on the mighty Lion of Judea."

"I did not 'pick' on him. He fell into the category of unelected rulers who left indelible imprints on the sands of time in their respective nations."

"Surely, you must know that the man is a god, the prince of princes, the Rastafari himself. As a doctoral student of politics at one of our prestigious universities, you should have known that you would be offending those who worship him."

"Do they really *worship* him? That's news to me." Chrys's tone was condescending, and it revealed a tinge of anger. "To answer your question, the man *is* not a god. I don't think anybody regards him as such. He was as much a god as every human being made in the image of the Supreme Spirit, the Formidable Force of Creation. I wrote about a man of great importance, an Ethiopian emperor, an unelected albeit popular politician, and an African statesman, not about his spiritual significance to Caribbean Islanders." Chrys was on the roll. He was about to throw all caution to the wind when he observed that the hostess was not listening to him. He stopped. He looked up and saw a group of people trooping in.

Rastamuffins!

20

"Cut! Cut!" the program director yelled.

"I'm sorry," Glory said to no one in particular. "I invited them." As the men took the vacant back-row seats, she walked up to them. Numbering about twenty, they were all tall and lanky, with long hairs tucked into large caps of green-yellow-red on a black background. Some wore large, leather Map-of-Africa medallions. Glory came back. "Collins, can we continue from where we stopped?" she called out to the director without asking why they were allowed to troop in while she was recording.

"Sure." The scruffy director adjusted his baseball cap and made signs to the cameramen. "Take two. Three, two, one and... ACTION!"

"But surely, Mr. Cheemay, you should have known that the Rasta movement wouldn't find it funny." The characteristic line of questioning triggered an animated applause from the men in long locks.

"Have you read the book, Miz Shantcross?" Chrys asked pointedly.

"Well, not all of it...."

"Then try and read 'all of it.' I don't see why you find it 'funny' and they can't. We cannot be too lazy to read and form opinions. We cannot rely on second-hand information, on self-appointed defenders of the faith we profess. You find them in every religion. I am here to tell you that I have written a book, not tell you 'all of it.' Don't believe the hype. Read the book." Chrys smiled as he managed to do some advertising.

"Surely, all those guys out there demonstrating can't be wrong. It is their religion, and it must be respected. It is morally binding on writers...."

"If I want to write a book about Rastafarians and they say the Lion of Judea is their G. O. D., I will note that point. What we have here is not a condemnation of Emperor Haile Selassie but a compilation of facts that would help people to understand his place in history. Why has nobody talked about the United Nations speech of 1968, which Bob Marley used in his epic song, *War*? It is there. I reproduced it."

"Then get together with the guys and sort out the problem. Actually, we have some members of the Rastamuffin community in the audience. Wouldn't it be nice if you talked about it and bring the unnecessary misunderstanding to a happy ending?"

Prolonged audience applause forced Chrys to switch to a combative mood, "What guys? What problem? Who has ever heard of Rastamuffins until now?"

The director made some sign and Glory appeared to understand what it meant. Chrys could care less; he had made his point. Glory cared; she had a career to build. It was obvious someone was not happy with something.

"I'm afraid I have to stop you here. We will continue the discussion after the break... to enable members of our audience to ask you some questions. Thank you very much. Ladies and gentlemen, the man of the moment: Chrys Cheekay Cheemay!"

Chrys walked out of the studio and saw Pete and Sean in the waiting room. "What are you two doing here?"

"Chrys, you are not being helpful. What do you mean by 'Don't believe the hype'? Hype, what hype?"

"Come on, Pete, it's not as if I discovered a cure for *dictatorisis*—the disease that causes dictatorship!"

"I know a high-street jeweller friend of my father's who could do with your services." Chrys didn't get it. Pete explained, "You are the only other person I know who puts down his product. Damn it, Chrys this venture is...."

"Stuff your venture, Pete. It's my head on the anvil. Let me tell you something, Mr. Publisher: I don't mind pure religious fanaticism; cannabis-crazed and drink-driven daredevils are a different ballgame. Did you see those guys in Channel EX documentary last Sunday?"

"Come on, Chrys," Pete said calmly. "Don't be unnecessarily paranoid. The lager louts were just having a good time and making the most of a chance to shine on the telly."

After a tête-à-tête with Glory, Chrys was introduced again. The Rastas in the audience were not Rastamuffins and had little objection to the issues raised in the book. Chrys was relieved and answered every question as calmly and as clearly as possible.

"Don't you think that what you wrote is tantamount to washing dirty linen in public?" a bespectacled Black lady asked.

"Ma'am, Henry VIII ruled England for 38 years. He had everything thrown at him: monstrous tyrant, bearded egocentric womaniser... and woman hater. The man might have been all that and more; I don't know. But...." Chrys paused to get the attention of everybody. "He founded a national church, a navy that ruled the oceans and, above all, he was the founder of the state you are a part of today. History judged him because the facts were there. I want you to judge these men by giving you the fat facts, not fancy fiction."

"Chrys," Glory began on first-name terms. "This Hastings Banda...?"

"*Ngwazi* Kamuzu Banda: President for life of Malawi, commander-in-chief of the armed forces, the minister for foreign affairs, defence, justice, agriculture and works and supply."

"Impressive. In your book, you suggested that the South African government sponsored the new capital at Lilongwe?"

"I did not. It's a historical fact that in 1967, Dr. Banda took the unprecedented step of establishing diplomatic links with the abhorrent apartheid regime in South Africa. When then Prime Minister John Vorster visited, he rolled out the red carpet. I avail the facts; you draw your own conclusions."

"But you painted him as presiding over a personal fiefdom?"

"Did I? Could Vincent van Gogh or Michelangelo have thought about the things said about their paintings? They were artists painting pictures, not the mega-million masterpieces we display today in museums. I set out like those great masters: no preconceptions, no prejudices, just simple facts of life."

"I have observed that most of your characters...."

"Subjects," Chrys corrected.

"Tend to keep it in the family," she continued regardless. "The ex-Christian Muslim, Al Hajj Albert Omar Bongo... his son Ali Bongo was a foreign minister."

"A post Pascaline Bongo has taken over."

"And another daughter, Albertina, is waiting on the wings. Is he lining them up for a Bongo-Bongo dynasty?"

"Maybe in an updated version, as hinted in the case of Equatorial Guinea President Teodoro Obiang Nguema, that question will be answered."

The taping continued with two female guests. One was a Birmingham-based novelist of Pakistani parentage. Born and brought up in Cape Town, Farrah Khan's novel dealt with the plight of women under apartheid. Titled *Cape Coloured*, it had been published in South Africa as two short stories titled "Amandla on Cape" and "Cape

Klerk." According to Miss Khan, "It tells how a coloured Capetonian couple made a mockery of the apartheid laws."

Glory introduced the third guest as if she were a Nobel laureate. "She is a renowned African-American poet, a social commentator, and an expert in political correctness currently sweeping across the world. Based in Harlem, New York, an activist and a community leader, ladies and gentlemen, please welcome my beautiful guest: Miz Yolanda Washington!"

Before she was asked the first question, Ms. Washington took Chrys up on a point she found "culturally cum sociopolitically objectionable. You suggested trivialization of women by the monarch in Mbabane. You forgot to highlight the tradition of the people and the customary connotations of choosing virgins for African kings."

"That's your own conclusion, ma'am. Using Henry VIII as an example, he sent two of his wives to be beheaded in the Tower. That did not detract from the fact that he was Catholic."

"Come on, brother; that was 500 years ago."

"Where I come from, there is a saying that whenever you wake up is your morning. So, for those of you shift workers, morning is in the mind." He paused for an animated, audience applause. "On a more serious note, choosing virgins for monarchs or crown princes is as old as civilisation itself. Not long ago in these lands, we had something similar. Everybody loved it and rejoiced with the royal couple. I wasn't writing about traditions. I wrote about individuals. With these facts, we can evaluate properly their eventual place in history vis-à-vis their contemporaries."

When two palm trees adjoin, their fronds abut, but Ms. Shantcross had a time-sensitive show to tape and Yolanda knew when to stop soiling the village spring.

109

21

Chrys met with Pete in the City of Westminster two days after the *Shantcross Show Special* aired.

"Seen this paper?"

Chrys took the obscure tabloid, *The Saturn*. "EXCLUSIVE—Overrated, Overhyped, and Over 'ere!" the front page screamed, and in smaller prints, "by the author himself." It took six reporters and additional materials from two subeditors to reproduce his interview almost word for word. "If this is journalism, God bless Great Britain."

"I warned you, Chrys; never put yourself down."

"Rubbish. It wouldn't surprise me if tomorrow I am spotted on the moon, near the Sea of Tranquillity, repairing a World War II bomber while sheltering in a London red bus! But this?"

Pete laughed. "Anyway, have you heard that Kenya banned the book?"

"Expected," Chrys said casually.

"And Zaïre?" Pete continued, visibly worried.

"They don't speak English; don't worry."

"Chrys, the French publisher already has a title: *L'état est moi!* or something. Zaire is a big market, and I intend to use it as a bargaining chip."

"Then don't. Sell him only the French translation for France. That will not include Canada's Quebec or any dependent Overseas Departments."

"You know I didn't think about that," Pete admitted.

"Good. So let's talk about serious issues. Have the Saudis said anything yet?"

"Why should they?" Pete asked instead. "We vetted out all mention of mad mullahs."

"Idi Amin lives there, that's why."

"Oh! I haven't heard anything from the Arab world." His mobile phone rang. "Excuse me. Yes?" He listened. "Just a minute.... You have a pen?" Chrys gave him one. "Oh, one more thing," Pete continued, after writing down some numbers. "Keep our man in Johannesburg posted. Bye.... No, I have an important meeting. It's all right, Marie. *Merci.*"

"Pete, you didn't tell me Pukemark has a South African rep?" Chrys said as soon as Pete stopped the annoying toy of yuppies.

"No, I am using Bolus facilities. Forget politics for a minute; let's talk commerce and raw economics. Can you think of any reason why they are developing cold feet?"

"I think the government wants to find out how the King of landlocked Swaziland will take it. You see, there are many siSwati in the country, and they are closely related to the Zulu. It's a delicate ethno-political terrain out there."

"So, what if the Old Shirburnian son of Sobhuza takes years to make up his virgins-powered mind, assuming he is interested?" Pete inquired.

"Tell the rep to release sample copies to test the political and economic waters."

"What if the demand is there? Copyright laws don't stand in the face of demand."

"That's your precious pot of porridge," Chrys offered with an air of resignation.

"Which reminds me, a bloke from your country sent in an order for... let me see, thirty thousand copies. I am shipping tomorrow."

"You can't do that, even if he pays cash."

"I don't see why not; it's called business."

"No, it's called breach of contractual agreement or some legal mumbo-jumbo like that. You sold the rights to Aladimma Books, remember?"

"Blimey! I forgot. On a happier note, the number of Caribbean countries banning the book has not increased as expected. The ruling Jamaican People's National Party is more likely to uphold the spirit of free trade than those socialist Labour Party."

Chrys laughed. "The Jamaican Labour Party is a party of the right. That's Edward Seaga."

"Labour everywhere is a party of pseudo-communists and their socialist bedfellows."

"In Jamaica, they are not. Michael Manley's nationalists are the socialists. Don't base your hopes on their right-wing credentials. Apropos, who is the Nigerian bookseller?" Pete fished out a card and gave it to him. "DOS INTERNATIONAL LIMITED, Importers, Exporters, Clearing and Forwarding Specialists, and International Linkages, Managing Director: Dayo Olaito-Savage, BA (Hons); LLB (Hons); MBA."

"It must be a big company." As Chrys let out a silly smirk, Pete added, "I still don't see why we can't sell to him."

Chrys deliberately ignored the first part of the question. "If he buys it here, fine; but don't export a page to Nigeria. You will be poisoning good business blood. Why do business with fly-by-night, gone-by-day, buy-and-sell cowboys?"

"Would you prefer Indians?"

Chrys laughed heartily as they walked down to the Tower tube station.

Chrys was in Oxford to see Pete the following week. They had lunch and talked about a new book tentatively titled *The Sandhurst Connection*, a study of some Sandhurst graduates and their role in coups d'état and countercoups all over the world. Pete would secure access to archived and classified materials. They shook hands on it.

"Another thing, these copies are to be signed."

"How many do I have to sign?"

"As many as possible," Pete said without looking up from some invoices. "The demand for autographed copies might increase, and I wouldn't have to call you."

While Pete swam in the high seas of wheeling and dealing, Sean stitched up deals that gave him instant returns. However, power of any shape or size intoxicates. Like many of Chrys's controversial characters, they did not know when to count their blessings and call it a day. Pete and Sean stayed on shifty sales, sketchy strategies, and shady schemes like white on rice.

22

Jahlove Rastaman was born Leroy Perry. His maternal grandmother brought him up after his unmarried mother speed-boated away with a beach bum. Perry never knew his father; his grandma died before he could ask. His natural locks stood him out amongst his mates. An English headmaster made the mistake of sending him home to have a "clean shave." Perry passed on education because certain natural signs should not be questioned. He grew up living a fancy-free-footloose life.

Perry became interested in Caribbean politics. A general election was due in Trinidad and Tobago. The campaign was fierce. The supposedly indigenous African citizens were out to ensure that their recent-immigrant Indian compatriots didn't snatch political power as well as keep tight fists on the economic pulse of the nation. He signed on as an activist. He was sent on a special recruitment assignment to Haiti.

After the election, officials turned their back on Perry. Perks pulverized. He had developed far above menial jobs. He had attended top party meetings, and he had seen how they did things. He could not take a backseat while the local politicians enjoyed the fruits of his labour. After all, his Haitian assignment was what won it for them. He approached a newspaper and sold the story. The publisher was a good party man; he promptly sacked the editor and apologised to the government. But enough had been printed. The minister of internal affairs arrested Perry before he could spend a penny of the 30 pieces of silver. He was to be deported back to Bermuda.

****

Back in Bermuda, the British colonial authorities heard about Perry. A meeting of the security committee determined that the news from Port of Spain, the Trinidadian capital, was not good: Perry was threatening to start a revolution.

"He will not find consumers of his gospel here," a local official suggested. The man should know; he grew up in the same neighbourhood as Perry.

"No, no," Sir David Smith, QC said in his characteristic Yorkshire accent. "We can't have him here. Send the lad away. Incarcerate him if he comes here." Her Majesty's Governor wouldn't know; he grew up thousands of miles away in Bentley, England.

Sir David was ill-briefed. When the news hit town that Perry was persona non grata, people were angered. The government quickly climbed down, but they had made Perry's day. He arrived home a hero. Hamilton airport was packed with hundreds of cheering citizens. The scene, by Bermudan standard, was akin to a quarter of China's population at Beijing's airport. A group of ambitious politicians reinvented Perry as "the messiah, the one that has come to lead our people out of the ugly sore of 21st century slavery by a distant queen. He has ideas; he has dreams; and he has guts."

When easygoing but colonial-minded Sir David was inexplicably murdered on his expansive abode, some smart sod linked the assassin to Perry. The crank that shot the governor with a locally fabricated Dane was a loony lone ranger, but Perry's utterances were enough to convict him of inciting murder. The police arrested him and earned yet another embarrassing point. The London-based Amnesty International weighed in.

A secret deal was ironed out. Either Perry left Greater Bermuda voluntarily or he would be jailed for life. Perry still preached "Armageddon in Jah Babylon." The prospect of hellfire on the peaceful island and its tourism economy was not what ordinary people expected of a messiah. He was losing public support, but he had no way of knowing he had become a megalomaniac. Like all megalomaniacs, he did not know when to start searching for his black goat because dusk was fast approaching. His lawyer brought it home to him that the game was getting too grizzly and that someone was going to get his goat.

"Listen to me, Leroy; you start a revolution and our industry suffers."

"What industry, Mr. Lawyer man?"

"Tourism. Take a look at Haiti!"

Perry sat with his "council" and agreed to move over to a small uninhabited island and create a paradise from whence they would return after forty days and forty nights. They were still there, long after forty months had elapsed.

****

In July 1991, Perry heard about Rastamuffins and that he had become the leader of international Rasta movement, or so "a reporter from a big British tabloid" said. Perry had no designs on leading such a movement, but the reporter put him in the picture. "It is time you came and talked to them to make the demonstration peaceful."

"Me come to England? No, man! I don't want none of them politics over there."

"Listen, Mr. Rastaman, my paper will pay for everything. You will only attend a press conference and give us an exclusive interview."

The Bermudan authorities woke up after the goat had left the pen and alerted Home Office. Immigration authorities waited at Heathrow. Perry flew back to Bermuda on the next available flight. The Rastamuffins organised a demonstration at Westminster and attracted the usual strange bedfellows: Giro Anarchists, People Campaigning for All-Rights minus Asylum, Anti-Capitalist Neo-Communists, Free-Everybody Movement, Don't-Pay-Tory-Tax Protesters, etc.

It was late summer; people were still outside worshipping the August sunshine. The tabloids were selling more papers than the book. Front-page news was scarce. Knives were out for a cut of scanty scandals to keep the circulation war alive. It would not be many months more before the House of Windsor handed scandals on a platter of platinum to worldwide media.

Chrys followed the whole episode from the secluded quietude of Southampton. He refused a repeat of *Shantcross Show*. People were leaving for late summer holidays. It was the silly season once again. Chrys did not want to be the turkey of the time. The safety of Southampton was reassuring. Arinze was due in London the following week. He had assured Chrys that he foresaw no immediate danger to his person; however, he must lie low in case some crank with a hole in the head lost a nut-bolt assembly too many.

"I am not losing any sleep," he assured Arinze in Igbo. "This is either the drumbeats of demons or the chants of ants; whichever, it will blow over on its own steam."

"Then again, the whistling of winds sometimes signals the start of a storm."

Two weeks later, the antsy chants turned into an annoying cacophony.

23

"Hello?" His inside felt consumed by liquid fire.

"Chiké, it's me: Kev."

"Good morning. How are you?"

"Listen, we have a little problem here. I tried to reach you late last night." Chrys had gone to New York-New York Night Club in the City Centre with a few fair-weather friends. "Adaeze had a little accident yesterday."

"Meaning?"

"I mean it's nothing we cannot handle."

"Is she okay? What happened?" Chrys was now wide awake.

"She was shot at by some fleeing armed robbers and was...."

"Was? Give it to me, Kev; I can handle it."

"Calm down, Chiké. She is alive but...."

"But what? Then let me speak to her!"

"Please hear me out. She is sleeping."

"You mean she is unconscious?"

"The doctors say she will make it. She is in intensive care. I saw her a few moments ago." Silence. "Hello? Are you still there?" Chrys mumbled something. "Kay is okay; she was discharged almost immediately."

"My Kameme! What the hell are you talking about, Kev?

Kevin patiently gave him the full story.

One thing that kept coming to his mind was to head for Lagos with the next available flight, but Kevin had said his folks warned against it.

The phone rang again.

Arinze was on the line. "Chiké, I have just spoken with Amaka."

"Where are you, sir?"

"I'm at the Kellys."

"I'll be there within the hour." Chrys tried hard to clear his conscience of the gathering gas of guilt, but something still told him the shooting had something to do with the book. She had said the book was "double trouble," even before she read a line.

"Hi," Sean said as he opened the door. "I heard what happened."

Chrys was not in any mood for unnecessary pleasantries. He entered the large lounge. Pat was with the men. A lovely lady with a normally infectious and ready smile, she sat visibly shocked. Seamus was comforting her.

"Sit down, Chrys," Seamus said.

They reviewed all they had heard and compared notes.

"Chief, with all due respect," Chrys said, "I have to be there by her side. I understand people in coma respond to the voice and touch of loved ones."

"Did they tell you she is in a coma?"

"Sleeping or unconscious is the same side of the coma coin: She is locked away in another world."

"Chrys has a point there, Uncle Tony." Sean appeared to be his only supporter. Arinze ignored him.

"Tony, listen...." Seamus began to say.

"No, Jim; that's final," Arinze declared like a chief judge. "Chiké, no disrespect intended, but you are far too emotional. You will only get in the way."

"It's understandable; that does not mean I am not level-headed."

"Mr. Level-headed, how did you get here? By taxi! You call that level-headedness?"

"Desperate situations, sir, demand desperate solutions."

"Exactly!" Arinze was unimpressed. "Stay here. I insist."

Chrys let it be. As if to break the suffocating silence, he let vent to what had been troubling him since he heard the news: "I don't believe it was an accident."

Arinze smiled: "Me neither, but I need to tie a few loose ends before saying for sure that it was an assassination attempt."

"Why would anybody want to hurt my baby?" Pat sobbed.

"It has nothing to with the book." Sean sounded so sure.

Chrys asked for proof. Sean had none; he just knew.

Arinze was ready to leave for Lagos when Sue arrived from Liverpool. She came with Amina, who was not aware of the incident. Sue took it more calmly than her younger sister. She and her husband sat in the dinning area and had a tête-à-tête. Chrys wondered if he would ever sit with Gina and talk about their daughter without threats and four-letter swearwords.

As if he read Chrys's mind, Arinze said as he rose to go, "Chiké, call Gina and tell her Kameme is all right."

Chrys could not recollect details of the train trip back to Southampton; he was plastered. In the morning, he called Ossie, Pete, and a few friends. He ate something, poured himself a kill-hangover drink, and then called Canada.

"What's up, Chrys?"

"Listen, Gee girl, Amanda had an accident in Lagos?"

"What business of mine is it if she's *facking* dead?" The American TV influence on her English was strong.

"Kameme was with her. She is okay."

"Who's okay?" she blurted, breathing heavily down the line. "Listen, Chrys, and listen carefully: If anything happens to my Lucia Maria, ANYTHING, you are gonna wish you never met me. *Capito*?!"

"*Si, contessa*," he said sarcastically.

"Chrys, you're not listening to me." She switched to Italian: "I will have your balls in a vice and personally squash them if a single strand of my baby's hair goes missing. I warned you about the green-eyed monster. You won't listen; you never listen to me."

"I spoke with her. She is okay, okay?"

"Where is she?"

"She is at Maggie's."

"Give me the number now!"

Chrys gave it to her. "The country code is 234. Dial '1' for Lagos."

"I know the bloody codes," she snapped.

"*Arrivederci….*"

The next morning, Chrys called Ossie and Vanessa and kept them posted. He declined the offer to come up to London and stay with them. At ten, he called his parents. They restated that he must not travel. Amaka, Mrs. Arinze, had brought Kamemena back to Enugu on the orders of Gina. Late evening, he called Charles in New Jersey, USA. He was out; LeJeune said Sue had told them.

It was past midnight when Gina called. "*Allo, Chrys*?"

"*Si, Signorina Gina Giacomelli.*"

"Tell me, Chrys: What was that bitch doing with Lucia Maria in Lagos?" Gina went on and on, swearing and abusing him. When she expressed her wish that Amanda were dead and that they got back together for their daughter's sake, he pulled the line off the socket.

24

"*Komm in, Kris. Willkommen.*"

"*Guten Tag, Fräulein,* what's happening?"

"Jackie and Amin," Monika said as she walked back to the kitchen. "Jackie iz korrekt; dat man iz not good. Ve never get anything repaired. All he vants iz money every veek, right on zee dot." Her heavily accented Germanic inflection made it hard to know when she was speaking Deutsche or English.

Chrys listened.

"If you get another step closer, you won't know what hit you," Jackie yelled from inside her room in her typical mad-rage, metallic voice.

"I only *vant* us to talk about rent," a much more conciliatory male voice pleaded.

"I don't wanna talk to you, asshole; just buzz off!"

"A nice girl like you shouldn't be rude." It was more a request than a rebuke. Amin's Asian accent lent it such a melodious tone that it came out as a plea. "You *arr* like a sister."

Jackie retorted, "If you don't get out of here, I'm going to call the police and press charges."

"Amin, come down here," Chrys intervened.

"I didn't do anything," Amin protested as he came down the stairs.

Chrys knocked on Jackie's door. "It's me."

"Come in, it's open." She was going through a jumble of makeup items emptied on the bed. The silky smoothness of her skin was stimulating.

"What are you doing undressed like that?"

"It's my room and I'll bloody well dress as I like."

The lace, skin-tone Tonga briefs left little to the imagination; she might as well be without them. The same-design, colour-to-match bra had a delicate stretch lace top; its unpadded, front-fastening, half-moon cups allowed the lace portion half-custody of her boobs. He had always teased Jackie that she could do with a slice of silicone. What he saw several moons after was both eye-popping and mouth-watering.

To break the silence and to take his mind off the arresting essentials, Chrys said: "Amin meant no harm. He is a businessman with mortgages to pay."

"Businessman, my butt; sister, my foot!"

"Amin was born and brought up in Entebbe, Uganda."

"Even if he was dusted and dragged up in Enugu, Nigeria, the slumlord is not my brother."

"I'm not here for Amin."

"Good. Give me a minute." Chrys began to sit down on her bed. "Out in the lounge!"

"All right!" He picked up a pair of cloth-adhesive insert pads for extra uplift. "You don't need these any more."

"Chiké, OUT!"

Chrys opened the door to leave and mumbled, "Attila."

"Bob-o-fine! Other blokes would have told Amin where to shove his rent book; oh no, not our 'Author of the Millennium'!"

"Green in the eyes, are we?"

"Look who's talking… green in the eye? Ha!"

That was unnecessary, but Chrys didn't mind. Amanda's eyes made her special. He had insisted that she should not mask the contrast of her pupils with contact lenses.

Chrys took her to Over the Tops, a decent restaurant on St Catherine's Road, off the Cobden Bridge over River Itchen and just a mile away in Bitterne.

Since Chrys's book made it to the bestseller list, he had been asking Jackie out to celebrate. She had refused. When Amanda was shot, she lent a lukewarm shoulder of support. Surprisingly, she called Chrys that morning and agreed to do dinner.

They ate and talked about the book, how it was going, and what he intended to do after the sudden success.

"I am taking it in strides," Chrys chuckled. "For now, it is more fame than fiscal."

"And to think our breaking up made you take up the idea," Jackie offered.

"Correction: *your* dumping me."

"And you couldn't wait to be bewitched by Amanda Arinze. Men!"

"Woe-man: Bewitch me and be my witch tonight!"

They went to Martine, a nightclub in Eastleigh, and boogied past midnight. Jackie held down two bottles of Cava Brute. When the cold breeze of Parkway plains hit her on the way home, she succumbed to the allure of Lord Bacchus. Chrys drove straight to his house.

"I don't live here." She sounded hollow.

"I do. Come in and have a bite to soak the booze."

It was about 4 am. Chrys picked up the remote controls. He lowered the telly and pressed <CD PLAY> on the midi-set remote. Barry White took over the background with her favourite number: *You're My Everything*. From here, it was an express ride back to the Garden of Eden for yet another bite of the apple.

She stood up abruptly and went to the mirror.

"Come here, love, don't spoil it."

"I have to leave."

"At this hour… after I've downed a bottle of Liebfraumilch? It's Saturday. Let's have brunch and drive down to Lymington and watch the rich and famous yacht on Solent."

"No, you are going up to London."

"I can cancel. Sean seems to be taking the agent business too seriously."

"What about the party? You are the special guest."

"Ah, I almost forgot. Say, why don't you come along?"

"I've heard it said that when little Willie Wanker down there takes over, the big Milk Monitor up here goes on AWOL!"

"What do you mean?"

"Hello? You are married to a girl from the same State. Look, it was a nice evening, and we should have called it a day hours ago. Don't get me wrong, I enjoyed myself. They say stolen water tastes better; I am now convinced. I guess I was more willing than you, but next time I wouldn't want to be looking over my shoulder while I drink."

Jackie phoned the next morning: "Are you still at home?"

"I'm ready. Actually, I was going to call a cab. I will be coming back late on Monday and I don't want to be clamped."

"I can drop you off."

Chrys was surprised. "Great. You can use the car for the weekend and pick me...."

"I don't want to use the car. You can pick a cab when you come back, or walk back through St Denys."

Chrys called Vanessa before driving over to Jackie's place. He moved over to the passenger side; she took the wheel.

"Thanks for walking me home," she said as she pushed the stick back to <D>. The X-registered, 75cl automatic Fiat Strada lurched forward.

Chrys smiled. "I had fun, but I suspect the earth did not move for you."

"I don't want to talk about it."

"Relax, Jackie; don't be so bloody tensed up. What's the matter with you?"

They were under M27 Junction-5 Flyover, the no-man's land between Swaythling and Southampton Eastleigh Airport.

Jackie flashed a fake smile and pinched his knee: "I am sorry, lover boy; it's hormonal, I guess." It had dawned on her that Chrys could have made a world of difference in her life. She wished Amanda were a foreigner or of another Nigerian ethnic group. In fact, if Amanda had been from anywhere but Enugu and unrelated to her, there would have been no contest.

She stopped at the station and walked him to the platform. "About last night, the green-eye sally and stuff, I'm sorry; I shouldn't have." Jackie looked like she meant it. "I am sorry about the earth not quaking, but you did not have to call me 'Adaeze darling.' Your train is approaching."

Chrys completely ignored the rebuke for an understandable mistake, kissed her goodbye, and walked into the open door of Network-Southeast train from Poole. He could see Jackie driving down the A335, Wide Lane, as the train pulled away from Parkway. Chrys shook his head and mumbled, "Whatever makes women tick must be beyond the comprehension of mere mortals."

He had an uneasy feeling as the train sped past buildings he recognised in Eastleigh and in Winchester and then the glass house in Basingstoke. He felt as if he was leaving for good. Something about Jackie's attitude was odd, though it was a great improvement.

"Clapham Junction. This is Clapham Junction...."

25

Chrys did not turn up for the party. Ossie had to explain several times that Chrys was on his way. When Sean came to the party without Chrys, Ossie and Vanessa smelt something fishy. They phoned Southampton; he did leave the city. They called Kensington; nobody was there.

The next day, Sunday, Ossie informed Pete. They informed the police. They were told not to worry. An adult could not just disappear between Southampton and London. If anything had happened anywhere in the region, they would have known.

By Wednesday, it became clear that Chrys was missing. On learning that he authored the controversial book, the police called in Scotland Yard. Days dragged onto a week. The police had considered the fuss a tabloid hot-summer whirlwind in an inner-city bowl of baked beans. It did not blow over; instead, it was now a hurricane.

Ossie relayed the bad news to their homefolk. The media got the news, despite the police promise to keep the news wrapped up for awhile.

"Author of Controversial 'Dark Dictators' Missing!" a tabloid screamed.

"Author Kidnapped," another concluded.

"Wacky World Writer Missing," took half the entire front page of *The Scum*.

A broadsheet publication did a special report that contained details of the author's background and his full names: Chrysogonus Chikéluba Chimé. *The Scum* published an old photo of Chrys and Gina, and hinted at an Italian Mafia job. Another tabloid said he was air-freighted in a diplomatic crate to Zaire that weekend. The Rastamuffins retreated. It was no longer a question of book-burning and chanting of "No justice, no peace!" A man was missing. Nobody was sticking out his neck. All sorts of scenarios were painted and printed. Expert opinions were dozen-a-dime.

A group of authors organized a seminar on SCAM — the suppression of creative and artistic minds. Notable speakers included Sir Drew. Commentators and critics went for the book and brought out issues that never crossed Chrys's mind. The copies Chrys had autographed fetched five times the cover price. Pete mounted an exhibition of Pukemark publication, which included rushed translation of the works of some obscure East European writers.

With Chrys missing, an important question re-emerged: Who shot Amanda? At the back of her mind, she believed someone wanted her dead, from her father through Omar to an unknown rival for Chrys's affections. Official police report revealed that a bunch of daylight daredevil armed bandits shot its way out of a botched operation. She was at the wrong place at the wrong time. A crack team of Mobile Police, a Rambo-like police unit with weird military tradition, went after the rogues, caught them near Seme, a town on the Beninoise-Nigerian border, and mowed them down. There were no identifications, no addresses, and no known accomplices: Unknown armed robbers. Case closed.

Amanda had recuperated in Enugu. The December wedding approached. Nobody could say to the bride on her wedding day, "The groom is gone." Eventually, they told her. Amanda had to be placed under 24-hour surveillance seven days a week. Her protests went unheeded. She threatened to phone the British Embassy and to say she was being held hostage in a foreign country. In Nigeria of those days, any family could conveniently lock up one of its own until the president came crawling.

December 1991, Ossie and Vanessa travelled to Enugu. They cancelled their Caribbean cruise because, as Ossie put it, "When something much bigger than *nte* enters its borough, the pigmy cricket heads for the exit; it does not stand to ascertain the validity of the eviction order."

Amanda's brother Charles flew in with LeJeune. Her uncle Gerry O'Brien visited from Tripoli. Amina was flown in at the end of term, when it was decided Amanda should stay back in Nigeria. In London, Seamus helped to get the incident into *Crimewatch UK*, which did not normally do missing persons. One tabloid offered a £10,000.00 reward for information leading to arrest and conviction of the perpetrators. *The Scum* made it £20,000.00. Soon, the Xmas hype exploded. Santa season surfaced again.

What a difference a year makes.

Amanda took delivery of some personal items from Chrys's room. She read his dairy, and it reinforced her belief that he was not gone on his own accord. She was cheered up by his vivid account of their meeting a year earlier.

Vanessa spent Christmas Day with Amanda. They had all travelled to Umuchimé, a twenty-minute drive from the Coal City. It was a great family gathering. The elders decreed that the children should not be made aware of the situation. Everybody put on a good face and enjoyed the Christmas celebrations.

"Say, Mandy, what's in the ransom note everyone is whispering?" Vanessa asked as they sat on the balcony of Chief Chimé's country home watching as young girls danced in the village square.

Amanda explained: "Some crooks asked for four million naira."

"Four million naira! How much is that?"

"I am not sure; but, at twenty naira to a dollar, it's a lot of money."

"Sir Patrick was going to pay?" Vanessa probed.

"You know Chrys's father; he throws money at everything. In my father's books, you do not negotiate with terrorists. He contacted the CID and SSS, and the fraudsters were nabbed."

"Thank God," Vanessa exhaled "SSS? That's the Colonel's state security setup?"

"Yes, Colonel Omar. They didn't have a clue what Chiké looks like. The bastards were just cashing in to make some money. These 419-ners are a breed apart, a different kind of bastards—as Chiké would say. They are vermin that must be eradicated."

"I keep hearing of 419; what is it?"

"It's the criminal code for advance-fee, flimflam fraudsters of international dimension, daring cheats who stop at nothing to fleece unsuspecting but equally greedy geezers."

"So, as things stand now, we are back to square one?"

"Not really, 'Nessa," Amanda continued, realizing that she really wanted to talk. "Dad believes it has nothing to do with anybody in this country. In fact, he is sure it has everything to do with the book. The question is, how? He reckons it's none of the dictators he wrote about, and I am sure he didn't just walk away."

Chrys's disappearance brought the book back to the top-ten list, but it was short-lived. The recession was beginning to bite. The book was still banned in those countries where the dictators reigned supreme. Opposition campaigners used photocopies as their bible. It couldn't have come at a better time. A wild wind of change was blowing across the world. Every country wanted to get rid of its leader. The Brits forced out Maggie Thatcher. Russians chose Boris Yeltsin. Americans dumped George H. Bush, even though he won a war; they settled for a little known governor from America's outback state of Arkansas called Bill Clinton and his smart wife Hillary.

Three months later, very early in March of 1992, Amanda gave birth to twins. She giggled all day when she saw the bouncing babies. Nobody knew why. They thought she was suffering from baby blues induced by Chrys's continuing absence. She wasn't. Amanda remembered reading that the thermal condition of one's body before conception determined the sex of babies: warm, girl; cold, boy. Hers was not only warm, it was hot. It was not just after having a hot bath, but in a Jacuzzi of passion-fruit essence, not once, not twice, but for weeks. She was looking at the results: both boys.

About her husband, Amanda reasoned, "There is no way Chrys could abandon everything and just vanish from the face of the earth. He just can't disappear without a trace in 1990's England. *C'est n'est pas possible!*"

26

Amanda announced her intention to fly out to Europe. Chief Chimé bought her a first-class ticket. There were many hands to nurse the babies, with Chrys's mother in charge. Even if Chrys had not been missing, Amanda still needed to get out. The attention was beginning to suffocate her. Mrs. Chimé had shielded her during the worst period. At some point, she was kept under constant observation. Her father brought in his own pressures. Since they rediscovered each other, thanks mostly to Chrys, now Senator Arinze had been attempting the impossible: make up for over twenty years in one year. They had grown so apart a normal father-daughter relationship was almost impossible. She left Enugu for Lagos with her father; he was on his way to Abuja, the federal capital territory.

Maggie and Kevin came over as soon as they arrived. Maggie had since warmed up to Amanda. Arinze flew on to Abuja the next day. He called Amanda later, left his telephone numbers at Nicon Noga Hilton Hotel, Abuja, and promised to be back before she travelled.

Spending some time in Lagos cleared her head of postnatal pressures. There was not much to do when everyone was at work. She would walk down to the beach, to the quiet spot she had sat with Chrys, or take a boat to Takwa Bay and enjoyed the unspoilt beach. Evenings, she called Enugu and checked on the babies.

It was half past six in the evening. The last flight from Abuja had landed. Amanda had confirmed her ticket for the midnight flight out of Lagos. She wanted to travel that night. She opened an envelope the gateman had delivered earlier. It contained a cheque for £1000.00 with a simple note: *Buy the children something special. Always, Omar.*

Amanda had been particularly rotten to Omar. She had cut him off from his daughter Amina. She had never bothered to visit his children with Kevin's sister; she now had hers, and he sent something to help. She reached for the phone.

"Omar, you shouldn't have," Amanda protested.

"That's the least I could do."

"Omar, I hate to trouble you, but…."

"What is it, my dear?"

"Could you guys get my flight delayed, please?"

"How am I supposed to delay a scheduled commercial flight?"

Amanda cleared her throat: "You are State Security, and you ask me how you could stop a foreign plane taking off into our airspace?"

"*Wallahi tallahi,* I don't know if I should…. Okay, 30 minutes, no more."

"Smashing! Please give your boys a good description of me. That shouldn't be hard. Some placard-carrying zombie is not my idea of a red-carpet reception."

"I'll be there," Omar assured.

She turned around and saw her father walking in leisurely. "Dad, where have you been?"

"I went down to the Club to see somebody. I've been trying to get through that phone. Who is arranging a red-carpet reception for you?" She told him. "My dear, you can't do that. You do not have to fly out today, do you?"

"Yes, I have cancelled twice already. We have to talk."

Arinze ignored her and dialled Omar's number. His 2-i/c said he had gone out for an airport assignment. "Come on! Tell me whatever it is in the car."

He fetched his revolver and put on a fresh Biafran suit.

"What was it you wanted to talk about?" he asked as they drove past Bonny Camp.

"Jackie."

"Jackie who?" Somebody ran onto the road. He honked and swerved.

"Jackie is the daughter of Justice Onaga. He visited earlier today with his wife."

"Oh, you mean Ebere Onaga?" He told her the story. In a nutshell, Amanda was named after Adanma Arinze, the younger sister of his father, his favourite aunt, and the mother of Justice Cletus Onaga—Jackie's father. She knew all that. She wanted to know more about Jackie. "Why?"

"I want to understand the opposition: I just found out about her and Chiké."

"Hey, a man must kiss many pumpkins before the Princess."

"Dad!"

"Didn't Chiké tell you?"

"No."

"And you wanted to delay the flight because...." Arinze swerved to avoid a convoy of speeding army vehicles with lights blinking, horns honking, and sirens flashing.

"That's Omar, follow him," Amanda said, giggling like a school girl.

Arinze followed. The soldiers didn't like the imposing black Mercedes Benz tailgating them. There was nothing they could do about it; no common man would be so daring.

Omar jumped out of the Nippon, four-wheel drive patrol car, known locally as *ọchọzọ* (pathfinder). Arinze stopped. Omar recognised his car and walked up to him.

"Good evening, Honourable Senator, sir!" Omar saluted.

"Evening, Colonel. I called your office, but you had left," Arinze informed him.

"True, sir!" Omar turned to Amanda: "Madam, at your command."

"I'm sorry," she apologized. "I hope it wasn't too much trouble."

"No." Omar then lowered his voice and whispered into her right ear, "No man likes to be dragged off his wife just before midnight. The sergeant's bed was already squeaking."

"You mean your unofficial bed was busy?" she responded rather loudly.

Omar laughed heartily and, as if to gloss over the gaffe, he said, "Just come and see us when you come back. Come with Chrys; I know he's okay."

Amanda turned to her father. "Dad, don't worry about me. I'll be fine."

Arinze was tired, and he needed an early night. He would be early at the local airport to pick up his wife Amaka, who would be on the first flight from Enugu — now that Amanda was away — to reclaim her turf. Omar assigned a vehicle to escort him back to Victoria Island.

"One more question, Dad, before you go: Why are you not close to Justice Onaga?"

"Says who? Cletus is more than a cousin; he is a *brother*. My father sent us abroad so as not to disrupt our friendship. He elected to go to Cardiff."

"What about the wife, Professor V. O. Onaga? Why was she so cold to me?"

"Well, when the fowl farts, the ground becomes a nuisance. Let's just say that my face doesn't do much for Virgie Nebo. It's a long old story."

"Nebo? Is her middle name Obiageli? Was she at Oxford with you?"

"Yes, why?"

"Nothing, it's just a crazy hunch. Please take care, Dad; I don't want to lose you again." Amanda didn't know why she said that, but it cheered him up.

They hugged.

"You know, I was wondering why the tortoise gears up besides a river that swallowed an elephant: Is the cunning creature going swim across or just jump over the river? Now I see the determination of an Arinze. It surely does not take a village to smoke out a rat. There is one thing I have learnt in all my years in security business: Never step into unknown territories like an elephant; *tigbue-zogbue* is a madman's mantra because huffing-and-puffing accomplishes little. I recall your husband likened this brewed brouhaha to the chants of ants; *ugoli agbịsị*, he aptly said. My dear, keep your ears to the ground. It shall be well with you."

Omar escorted Amanda to the VIP lounge. He loved it because he wanted them to be friends. Marriage was never on the cards, especially after the scandal. Even then, Amanda had told him she was not born to marry a service staff: "Anyone who consciously signs his death warrant must have his head examined."

"Your Dad was worried by that question," Omar observed as they waited in the VIP lounge.

"He should be. You don't go dumping your sweetheart, a girl your dad selected as your bride and sent to Oxford, because she is too smart for a society that wants women as public trophies, good cooks, and whores in bed."

Omar did not know what she meant to convey. He let it slide. He did not want to spoil the quality time with the mother of his daughter.

The day John Major picked up the Tory blue torch and decided to give Neil Kinnock a run for his Welsh red rose, Amanda entered England. The election was far from her mind. She came determined and prepared to pick up the pieces of her life.

27

With wads of money, lots of free time, and family support, Amanda was determined to get Chrys out of whatever or whosoever held him incommunicado. She moved to Pat's and took over her former room, which Sean had turned into an office.

A week later, she travelled to Liverpool to see her mother. Sue was not thrilled to learn that she left Amina behind. Two days later, she left for Southampton. She had brunch with Ivy, Chrys's landlady. She was at Jackie's Granby Grove residence at lunch time.

"Can I be of some assistance, ma'am?" the bloke who opened the door asked.

"I am looking for Jackie."

"Wonder Woman! I didn't meet her. I think Monika can help you. Step right in."

Amanda had been there with Chrys to see Doreen. If anything, things seemed to be getting worse. She picked up an old copy of *Hello!* magazine. She browsed through the glossy colour photographs.

"Amanda!"

"Hello, Monika."

Jackie had moved to Montefiore after the quarrel with Amin. She paid him all right, but she left unpaid phone bills big enough to ensure that British Telecom severed services. Doreen had also moved.

"It's a shame what happened to Chrys," Monika said after the situation report.

"Thank you. Where in Montefiore is Jackie staying now?"

"She stayed in B Block, but she has moved again. Check her department. Please, let me get you a cup of coffee."

Amanda was surprised that Monika had almost lost her strong German accent. It was still there, but she now pronounced English words distinctly.

As Monika prepared coffee, she flipped through the phone bills. Some numbers were familiar. She removed her glasses and looked again. Her aunt's London number and several 010-234-42 numbers were prominent. Of all the international calls, none was to the Chimé residence. She took the phone bills and put them in her in bag.

On her way to the campus, she saw a girl with long, flame-red hair coming out of the Electronics Building. Her pace was deliberate, as if she was counting. It could only be one particular person in the whole wide world.

"Dor!"

"Mandy!" She ran across the barracks-gate barrier and embraced Amanda.

"Look at you... flaming freckles farm!" Freckles literally grew on Doreen.

"I am planning to patent it. Look at you: glossy gold, full frontal, and ever exotic! Say, what is the situation?"

"We are still waiting and watching. Everybody has been supportive. Seen Jackie O lately?"

"Say, is there a Nigerian hobby like 'putting people down'?"

"I hear you can't stand her."

"I can assure you, Mandy, the feeling is mutual."

They walked to Union Building, bought drinks, and went into West Common Room.

"Mandy, if you're looking for aggro, you have come to the right place. Jackie O has no respect for anybody. I don't think you are in her Christmas card list."

"Dor, I didn't travel thousands of miles to enlist. I just want to talk with her."

"She's so bloody cocky you want to bash her head in. If she were Indian, she would be a four-legged goddess: She's a flaming cow, an Amazon from Hun."

At the Staff Club taxi rank, she gave a Basset address.

"You may want to walk. What I mean, ma'am, is that Pansy Road is just across Burgess Road, off Honeysuckle. Once you get to the Post Office on Dahlia Road... opposite the bank, the street is spot on. You can't miss it."

"I think that is why some smart sucker invented taxis."

The house was like any other around the area. The tree shadows from Basset Green provided a welcome shade that made the atypical hot sunshine milder. There was no doorbell, just an antique metal knock.

"Hello?" A short, slim Chinese girl opened the door.

"Hi, I'm Amanda. Does Jackie live here?"

"Lynn Li, who is it?" The assertive voice of Jackie was unmistakable.

Amanda stepped in. The lounge was tastefully furnished and well-kept. The live-in landlady took good care of the property. She sat down and leaved through Jackie's final-year thesis.

"Adaeze, *kedu*?"

"*Ọ dị mma.*"

"Welcome."

"Thank you. Your parents came to see me in Lagos. They are doing extremely well."

"I heard."

Gradually, the discussion came to the expected edge.

"As you know, I am looking for Chiké."

"I sold the car and gave Ossie the money."

"It's okay. Did Chiké tell you anything to suggest that he was not his usual self?"

"No, Amanda, I don't recall."

141

"Jacqueline, please," Amanda said, matching her mood swing by adopting her real name. "He must have said something. Okay, I've been talking with Doreen; she...."

"Imagine being saddled with such a name from men's magazine. What has the tart to say about me that I haven't heard?"

"I am not interested in your petty problems. As I was saying, she saw you and Chiké at the club. I was hoping that... since he spent the last night here with you...."

"Did Do-or tell you that?"

"She didn't mean to suggest that he *spent* the night with you or whatever. He wouldn't do that. Besides, that would be quarrelling over the shadow of an ass."

"He wouldn't?" Jackie mumbled almost inaudibly.

"I believe there is something he said that night. You know he is always making silly remarks. I am looking for clues, damn it."

"I don't want to talk about Chiké with you, not today, never. If it makes you feel good, I will say you won the war. Why lose the peace by exhuming dead bones."

Jackie was insensitivity made flesh; Amanda could no longer restrain herself. "A guy you loved goes missing and you talk about dead bones? What is eating you that you are turning into an insufferable bitch? Remember that a river that forgets its source dries up."

"Go ahead and insult me. The Do-ormat said I am a cow; what's new?"

"And you said she is 'a dejected daughter of a demented dog'; what's new?"

"That junk-heap tramp; if I didn't separate her head from her body, it was because I know where I am going."

"I wonder where?" Amanda interjected dryly. "Look, let's keep Doreen out of it."

"I don't trade insults, my dear. The hawk and the vulture do not scramble for food."

"The vulture is a scavenger, and the hawk is a predator. And?"

"There is such a thing as breeding, not brought-up; class, not circumstances. Do-or does not know that there is trash and there is trashy trash!"

Amanda knew when to stop trying to squeeze juice out of a plastic. No one swallows phlegm to appease the pangs of hunger.

As she walked down Burgess Road, something struck her. She walked through the University towards Granby Grove. She saw Monika walking up the street.

"Did you succeed?" Monika asked.

"Basically, yes. There is something I forgot to ask you: Doreen and Jackie?"

They were not the best of friends, Monika opined, but they got along well. After the drinking binge at a party in London, she asked Jackie to help her find an abortion clinic.

"What actually happened?" Amanda probed.

"I think Doreen found out that Jackie had used that clinic. I observed changes in her... boobs?"

Amanda nodded.

"She became moody. She had a terrible quarrel with Chrys.... Oops, I don't think I should be telling."

"It's all right, Monika. That was before we met."

"Good. Oh, it was Doreen who told Jackie she saw Chrys and a woman."

"That was his cousin Adaora."

"He told you? So if Jackie didn't want Chrys to know, Doreen knowing lets the cat out of the bag. I think Doreen didn't know about abortion being taboo in Jackie's society. Jackie was mad. Maybe Doreen told her boyfriend Sean, or Jackie knows some secret about her. I do not know. Jackie is not one to talk anyhow; she is basically a nice girl. Doreen is not bad, but she is not very mature."

Amanda could only guess what went wrong: "It must be a man, but not Chrys. Whatever it is, it has no direct bearing on my quest."

Amanda took a taxi from where she had taken one an hour earlier.

"You again," she said on recognizing the driver.

"Same profession, same place... different times," he replied and readied himself for a relatively longer trip.

"Parkway, please."

28

Amanda made little progress. Every lead led not far or to nowhere. She drove to Oxford and listened to Pete give her a breakdown of how well the book was doing. Some funds were built into shares for Chrys, and he had moved some money into *The Lords & Commons*, the news magazine he had launched.

"Pee, please, I am neither interested in the book nor the money. I just want to know what you have done about my husband's disappearance."

"I am sorry, Mandy, but there is nothing anyone can do now except hope that he is okay. I have pledged to pay £20,000.00 to anybody who can help. Between us and these four walls, I am ready to pay out that money as ransom."

"It won't be the money a certain tabloid pledged?"

"Well, we all chip in. I have been working closely with *The Scum*."

"Before or after his disappearance?"

"Long before... since the Rasta blokes took to the street." Pete was not sure if he should have said that.

"Did Chrys know you were working with *The Scum* to promote the book?"

"You know how Chrys feels about tabloids. Okay, some are terrible trash and all that, but it is business and nothing else. I am not interested in their junks either. You know what I mean."

"The things money make people do," Amanda mumbled.

"Sorry?"

"Nothing. I must be going."

At the Kellys, Amanda announced at breakfast that she was flying out to America to see Charles and LeJeune.

In the plane, she reflected on what she knew so far. Somehow, Sean and Pete appeared to avoid discussing Perry. She had gone into his room and watched video tapes of Chrys's interviews and news items on the Rastamuffins. Somehow, Sean cropped up in the background of the first demo. The Sally Ann report showed Sean giving her the book. He must have gone to the television studio to procure that particular tape. He knew they were hiding something. She would get it from the source: Leroy Jahlove Rastaman Perry.

"Call us as soon as you settle down," LeJeune said as they saw Amanda off at JFK three days after arriving New Jersey from London.

"If you don't call by the weekend, I'm coming out there," Charles told his sister. He was looking more like some Sicilian playboy; LeJeune, like the wife of a banana-republic dictator, a Bay Watch babe with brains.

It was an early morning flight, so Amanda had the whole day ahead of her.

"Jahlove Rastaman? Just get to Castle Harbour and take a boat." The guy sounded so casual she looked stupid for asking.

Ten kilometres away, just across Harrington Sound, she paid the driver and walked down to the beach. Some locals milled around what looked like an office.

"Good day, folks," she said respectfully. "How can I get across this stretch of water?"

"I won't say you walk, unless you be one of them apostles of Jesus," one said and let out a loud burst of laughter. Others didn't enjoy the joke. The man was unshaven. His spitting did not bother her, but the copious amount of phlegm produced was gross.

"Funny!" Amanda said and grinned mechanically.

After negotiating her fare, the speedboat took off. The driver talked his head off, when he was not singing some calypso tune that was both sexist and pornographic. It was a lovely cruise, but Amanda hated being in a metal contraption of any size on a large body of water.

Perry's base was in one of the north-western, low-lying coral islands. It provided a safe haven for all sorts of people who want to lie low. It was easy to locate Perry.

"Ah, our Lady Londoner asking about me in town!" Perry chuckled.

"Hello," she greeted. "I was only asking for directions."

"Don' matter... don' matter at all. Sistahs like you are welcome here anytime. Come here, sit down. Wilder, get the lady something to drink, man."

Amanda accepted the drink out of politeness. When she took a sip, she knew what it was: a coconut-flavoured rum concoction called "Coco Corumba."

"So, what brought you all the way from Queen's country?"

"Your industry: tourism," Amanda answered.

"I've heard that before. We're some window showcase them come to look at, but when I go to them over there, I'm not welcome." Perry did not only sound knowledgeable about his little Rastadom, he knew the history of Bermuda. He told Amanda its recent history from the arrival in 1515 of Juan de Bermudez, after whom it was named. "Then came folks from England in 1609 and, before you know it, bingo, you have the oldest colony of Britannia! Hundreds of coral islands, that's what them say them saw. We never existed; we still don't exist."

Every country deserves its government, or so Amanda believed. What Perry had to say about Bermuda

147

was irrelevant. She had to address the personal issue that brought her out there. From further discussions, she found out that Perry had little knowledge of the Rastamuffins or of any international Rasta federation.

"Listen, sistah, I don't have water in me mouth. Read me lips: Rastamuffins don't exist. Some people are out to give Jah Rastafarian a bad name. By the way, why are you asking all them questions?" She told Perry that she was working for the wife of the author who went missing many months before. "I'm sorry to hear that. This guy came over, gave me a copy of the book, and said if I come over I could help stop them burnings." He narrated his truncated-travel experiences. "I found nothing wrong with the book. The writer said nothing about Rastas."

"What's his name... the reporter?"

"A young man of about twenty five or so, not more, with jet-black hair, too dark for them English men... I don't remember his name. Mr. Paul or Patrick or Peter, but it starts with a 'P.' Smith or something is the surname, I can't remember.... Aren't they all Smith?" Perry joked, an unveiled reference to the slain governor.

"Thank you, Jahlove, for your time. Please accept these gifts as a token of my ample appreciation for your candid cooperation." She was beginning to sound like Chrys and she hated it.

Perry accepted wrapped gift. He thanked her and said he wasn't expecting anything from her. He didn't know what it contained, but the wrapping alone was great. He escorted her back to the boat, where the guy who brought her was waiting.

"You take her nice and easy back to Hamilton, man," Perry told him. He nodded. "Which reminds me, before I make the mistake all over again, what's you name?"

"Ann."

"Ann who?"

"Onymous," Amanda added.

"Ann Onymous, huh?" It didn't sound right. It was familiar, yet strange. In his travels up and down the western waters that defined Caribbean Sea as a different body of water from Atlantic Ocean, he had heard names that were out of this world. "Okay, Miss Ann...."

Amanda knew the sooner she left the place the better. At the hotel, she called Charles in New Jersey. They were not at home. She left a message. "Charlie, LeJeune: I'm coming back tomorrow morning," she said after the long tone. "Please wait for me at JFK. Check the flight schedules."

On Friday, April the 20th, as John Major was taking up residence at No. 10 Downing Street for full five years of trying to be his own man, Amanda flew into London. She bought a copy of *The Lords & Commons*, Pete's venture into the popular political press. Occupying a quarter of the front page of that special edition was a colour advert for limited special edition of "L & C's Book of the Year."

Amanda had always felt that Pete was putting excess energy into the book. She felt there was more to it than money. She asked Seamus to get her everything on Sir Drew. Her hunch was right on the money: The man had lost a lot of money to indigenisation policies of some African countries. It was nothing personal, but his interests in some multinationals were eroded. His South African interests were sound, but that didn't mean he was for apartheid policies—in his books.

Amanda was none the wiser about Chrys's whereabouts, but she had realised that "man is basically a selfish animal." She thought to herself, "There is always some sinister and or selfish motive lurking behind every move of man. It is possibly subconscious, a survival instinct." Chrys had tagged a very fanciful phrase to her wanting to hurt her father: Belated blighted blues, he had written in his diary. "Blues, yes; even belated, but blighted? Now, what would he call Sir Drew using his son's venture to get even with the dictators that rubbed him wrongly? Blighted blues, in Chrys's book, must be a euphemism for vicious vengeance, rabid revenge, or getting one's own back. Assuming Pete is fronting his father's revenge, what subconscious selfishness laid Chrys open to such a manipulation? How does Sean fit into the jigsaw puzzle? And Jackie?"

Amanda thought so hard and long she felt disgusted with humanity. There were so many questions and no single straightforward solution. She decided to get Chrys out first and then worry about the underlying motives. To do that, there was one open lead left to tug: Sean.

29

Amanda confronted Sean and threatened to go to the police. He confessed: "Pete invented the Rastamuffins. They don't exist. He paid people to put on wigs and chant. He didn't let me in on it until some guy made away with a day's payment. The whole thing was crumbling when he found out about Perry. Lady Beth of Bermuda, Sir David's widow, and Lady Anne, his mother, are cousins."

"And Project Perry was hatched," Amanda concluded. "Pete flew out to Bermuda as 'Peter Smith,' a reporter, and made Perry come over to incite the real Rastas. I know all that. What I want to hear about is 'Project Prisoner,' your baby."

Spurred on by the Perry project, which was Pete's idea from A to Z, Sean designed his own scheme without telling Pete. He brought in two Welfare weasels, Joe Watson and Doyle O'Donegal. They tricked Chrys to a disused basement office. He was held there for some time.

"When the money started coming in, some other characters hijacked the project. They moved to where I do not know."

"So why not release him now that the book is off the bestseller list?"

"The paperback is due to be released in America next week. The British paperback has been postponed; Scotland Yard says a paperback here might jeopardize Chrys's safety."

"You realize it is my husband you are messing with, a guy who trusted you so much. Listen!" Amanda demanded as Sean began to speak. "What effect would the American publication have?"

"They reckon it will bring the book back on the list here, thereby renewing their income."

"And if the book breaks the 200 record appearances that Stephen Hawking's *A Brief History of Time* is bound to do, then what?"

The story did not sound right. Joe and Doyle were not that sophisticated. Sean seemed to be lying to buy time. Amanda was getting furious, and her face was turning deep red with rage.

"They now want a lump sum in lieu of expected revenue from projected sale increase."

"And you can't deliver the ransom without raising eyebrows. You can't go for *The Scum* money; you can't go to Pete either. Now, let me ask you one question: Have you told them that kidnapping is a serious criminal offence?"

"They know. They reckon Pete and I are in it. The last thing any of us would want is a scandal, especially with Sir Drew and Dad in the public eye."

Amanda managed a smile. "So they have it all stitched up. Any phone numbers?"

"No, they call every Friday evening at nine… at a different designated public phone. They tell me by mail within the week which phone booth they'll use."

Amanda was in a square that had lost a side. As long as she kept the other sides from coming together to form a triangle, she would succeed. She had to be one step ahead. She demanded for details of Sean's initial scheme. Sean parted with the Brixton address.

Late that evening, Amanda complemented her pair of jeans with one of Chrys's shirts. She put on an old leather jacket and a beret. She drove to the South London address.

As she stepped into the basement office, a certain cold feeling engulfed her. The place was damp and stale, a functional junkyard. The double-drive PC that sat on the table hummed like a small engine starved of air. She sat on the creaky swivel chair. She reached for the on-off switch. Silence. Then the door groaned and moaned as the smallest whiff of breeze squeezed past. Nothing looked normal. Dust hung everywhere: dust seen, dust tasted, and dust smelled. There were cobwebs too.

Dejected and disappointed, she decided to leave. She heard approaching footsteps and she hid behind the door. The moment she always dreaded was come. The man had a female partner. She wiped her wet forehead with the back of her left hand as the smell of fish and chips and vinegar hit her nose. The couple had come to stay. She made an eerie noise and increased the intensity briskly. On hearing running footsteps, she walked out immediately.

"Told ya," the skinny girl with matted, peroxide-blonde hair said as Amanda walked past them near where she had parked her car. The girl was still panting, shaking with a spasm of fear so intense she drank from a bottle to calm her nerves. "Told ya, Mickey: the 'ouse's 'aunted!"

Back in Kensington, she discarded the plastic gloves, the type that look like condoms for a baby octopus. She watched some television to relax her nerves and slept on the sofa.

The phone woke her up; she had a giant headache. She raised her hand; it was heavy, no thanks to her awkward sleeping position. Somehow, she reached for the phone just before it stopped. She depressed the speakerphone.

"Yes?" Amanda hated her voice.

"Hi darling, it's me. Are you okay?"

She reached for the receiver. Only two people called her "darling." God, let it be Chrys, she prayed. "Yes?" She tried to shake her brain into working properly and quickly.

"Are you okay? I phoned Enugu...."

"Uncle Gerry! Where are you?" she said, happy but disappointed.

"Still in good old Muammar's Jamahirra! Anything new and different?"

"Yes, but I can't speak here."

"You are speaking!" Gerry joked.

Gerry agreed to meet with her the next day in Sliema, just across Marsamxett Harbour and a bus-ride away from Valletta, Malta. Amanda fixed herself a strong cup of coffee, liberally laced with Irish cream. The concoction gave her a better, stronger, and more pleasing kick than Perry's "Coco Corumba."

She was on her way out the next morning when the phone rang. It was Sue. Pat had told her that Amanda was going to see Gerry. Amanda ignored the call. She walked out of the room. The call would have saved her the trip.

30

Named after Jean de la Vallette, the Grand Master of the Order of Knights of St John to whom Malta was ceded in the 16th century, Valletta was a city that strived hard to enjoy the economic prosperity of its European political partners while clinging to the exoticism of its African-Arab cultural cousins.

"Glad to see you again, darling," Gerry said as she alighted from the bus.

"Look at you, Uncle Gerry: You look like a sheik!"

They had supper at a local eatery.

"What's this stuff called?" Amanda asked.

"Taramasalata. It's Greek," Gerry explained.

"It tastes Greek too; it sounds Italian though."

They walked back to the hotel and ordered drinks. He had stout beer; she, Lambrusco Rosé. Amanda told Gerry all about her effort to get to the root of Chrys's disappearance, her trip to Bermuda, Sean's role, and what she was planning to do to Joe and Doyle.

"What sort of cowboy commerce is this? I bet your husband will spit hot pebbles when he finds out."

"He'll be all right. He has a wacky sense of humour. I hate to say this, but their originality is overwhelming."

"Originality? Smart, yes; original, no. Can't you see it is a copycat?"

Amanda did not have to think about it. Probably, she sowed the seed that sprouted and grew into a bush. Cold sweat appeared on her forehead. "It is definitely not a first, but proper people do not deliberately invent controversies."

"Ben Johnson was right," Gerry continued. "If my memory serves me right, it was he who wrote and I quote: 'Few attacks make....' No, 'Few attacks, either ridicule or invective, make much noise but by the help of those they provoke.' You get it?"

"Ben Johnson said that?" Amanda asked with unmasked scepticism.

He looked bewildered.

"Get the mosquito off your ears, Uncle Gerry! I was pulling your legs; actually, it was Samuel Johnson you quoted."

He sat back.

"My forefathers put it more succinctly: 'Not every speech deserves a response.'"

"That's not an Irish saying," he observed.

"Aye, my forefathers were Igbo!"

"*Mais oui!* Sean and company are treading on the well-ploughed field of human gullibility. So, what is it about Liam O'Donegal?"

"I was thinking you could get him to pull his nephew off the case."

"Mandy darling, Liam is bad news. He is a specialist in subtle racketeering. I won't tell you what, but he is not involved. Doyle is not smart enough for Liam's thingamabob. The Joe character is equally unsophisticated. Liam is more an adjunct IRA operative than a crook. You involve Liam, and he'll take over. What began as a joke would assume professional complexion. Go for Doyle. Get the vagabond and make him sweat."

"He is a dead fowl the moment I set eyes on him."

"Don't approach it like that. You must be coolheaded; otherwise, you will make mistakes. The whole thing could blow open. Pat will never forgive you two if you drag Seamus into it, and I don't want her hurt by the childish pranks of an overgrown nipper." A chemical engineer, Gerald O'Brien lost his wife to breast cancer and had not remarried. He was over-protective of Pat, his twin sister. His special love for Amanda derived from Pat's affection for her: the daughter she always wanted, the daughter she never had.

"One last thing, Uncle Gerry: Why would the two bandits still sign on for the dole if they are creaming off enough money from Sean?"

"Penny, love. The problem with such guys is that no matter how much they get, they still sign on for extra freebies."

Pennylove, Amanda thought as the bus pulled away, the love of money.

Back in Britain, she took a shower. Wet hair wrapped in a towel and a glass of Bailey Boo in hand, she sat on the floor and began to call everybody who had tried to get in touch: Pat, Adaora, Ossie, Sean, Sharon, Doreen, etc. She replaced the handset to get a dial tone for another call. The phone rang. Pete.

"Mandy, I've been calling you since yesterday…. please hear me out. I have nothing to do with the recent episode. I admit I should have told you about Jahlove Perry. I've put a cheque in the post to cover the cost of your trip. I insist, please. I'll pull out Chrys's money from the paper and you can have it."

"Are you folding up L & C?"

"The old man says I should sell. The House of Lords is a morgue of weirdoes. The House of Commons will become a college debating chamber with Neil Kinnock and Maggie Thatcher gone. The Maastricht Treaty debate didn't explode as expected, and the new MPs are towing the government line as though we're in communist China. The Tories are going down for a long count. It's the magic of Maggie, a curse."

"Don't worry about the investment; some go top, some go pop. Chrys would understand."

She called Sue, whose Liverpudlian life had been rearranged since Amina left the nest. Amanda did promise to return Amina as soon as she had soaked up enough convent discipline with Kamemena, as dished out by her mother-in-law. With Sue, she would still be Grandma's girl who was terrified of spiders on television. In Enugu, arachnophobia was an affliction of wimps.

They talked about her trip to Malta.

"You had to fly out to Monaco for 'uncle-niece stuff, family, weather... the usual things'?"

"Malta, Mom, not Monaco. It's cheaper, come to think of it. You need to see my telephone bill. Speaking of which, I'll speak with you again tomorrow. Goodnight, Mom." Amanda was about to drop the phone on her mother, who really wanted to talk.

"One last thing, Amanda Arinze, please tell Sean Kelly to get Doyle O'Donegal off my back, or I'll get the police to do it. What sort of business is Sean into that Pat doesn't know about? I hope he does not take the flash-pan agent business seriously."

It was Sue who dropped. Amanda clutched the receiver, teeth clenched and unable to speak. Angry, she screamed and flung the phone across the room.

31

Amanda was so sick of Sean's lies she decided to sidetrack him. She tracked down Joe at a Peckham snooker club, where he was taking money off some suckers. She took him to the bar and bought him a pint. He guzzled it as would a radiator deprived of its fluid on M25, Britain's busiest thoroughfare. She bought him another.

"Okay, Joe. The job, let's hear it."

"What job?"

"What job?" Amanda mimicked. "Sean's job."

"Oh that! It's over. They paid; I walked. That Tory boy from Oxford tried to be smart. He's lucky *The Scum* reporter refused to pay. How am I supposed to get 'concrete evidence' for pennies; know wha' I mean?"

The confession confirmed that Pete bankrolled the publicity stunt, which was why Sean ran to tell him that she was onto them. Joe was sweating, his stained shirt smelled of stale sweat, light lager, and cheap cigarettes.

"Okay, what about your uncle's studio in Brixton?"

Joe looked surprised. "I don' know what you talking about, Miss Mandy. We used the place during the Rastamuffin days. The house is haunted at nights; no one lives there."

"Don't get smart with me, Joe; I could have you in the nick within the hour."

"Since you helped us with Grandma coming over for that eye operation last two years, have I ever told you any lies?"

Amanda had worked with the Citizen Advisory Bureau. Mrs. Watson was so pleased with the help she invited Amanda to a thanksgiving service the Sunday before Grandma Watson returned to Jamaica. She took

Sean along, and that was how he met Joe. When Sean got the agent job, he phoned Joe and Rastamuffins were invented. "Okay, Joe, have another beer and let's hear it minced and microwaved." She was past playing games, and she was not interested in his latest-craze, board-game haircut. But Joe was done.

Amanda had told her mother to pay Doyle up to a certain ceiling. That was a mistake. As she discovered in Liverpool, the 'ceiling' was enough to send Doyle to Brighton. She took another train down south to Brighton and combed the beaches. It was the second May bank-holiday weekend. By Sunday, she did what she should have done.

"Mrs. Watson? It's Mandy from CAB, remember me?"

"Of course! How are you, my child? I heard you left the country."

"Yeah, but I am back. Please, is Joe there?"

"No, but I can send for him," Mrs. Watson offered.

"Thank you. I'll call back in an hour."

Joe was waiting when Amanda called again. She asked the questions; he had the answers. "Joe, please listen carefully: I don't care what it takes, keep him there!"

"You mean it, Miss Mandy?"

"'Have I ever told you any lies'!"

The next train out of Brighton was in five minutes time. She had checked out of her hotel. She had no luggage. She only carried cash cards and IDs. Her jeans had accumulated so much dirt she decided she would throw the pair away. Her underwear garments were now disposables.

The train was ten minutes late, but it made up for the tardiness. They were in London on time. She took a black cab to Peckham. Doyle was in the club guzzling Guinness.

"Miss Mandy, that will be twenty quid, know wha' I mean?" Joe was grinning as if he just won a triple stake.

Amanda gave him £25.00. Joe produced a wider grin. She turned and faced Doyle. He recognized her. "Hi, Doyle, remember me? I believe you have something to tell me."

It was already seven o'clock, but it was still daylight. They walked across the street and took a cab to Holland Park.

"Now, Doyle, I want you to tell me everything you know about the job."

"Why should I?" He had taken in some fresh air.

"Simple: Uncle Liam is waiting across the street to beat the crap out of your dickhead." Amanda was past pussyfooting.

"Liam O'Donegal?"

Yes! You can't go about taking hostages and expect him not to hear."

"But Mandy, you should 'ave asked me first."

"I am asking you!"

Between loud burps and hiccups, it emerged that Sean told him to meet Chrys at Waterloo. He did. They took a cab to Brixton. That was his assignment. Some guy took over. They left in the guy's car. "He...your man... asked him... the other guy. He... the guy... said Tooting Bec or Broadway... I am not now sure. He's not as tall as your man, darker… not as heavy either."

"Are you absolutely sure?"

"I was there!" Doyle declared. "Sean didn't pay up. I told your Mom; she paid up."

"Didn't you hear the police were looking for my husband?"

"Never!" he swore.

Amanda went over to Pat's place to freshen up. She was in her bedroom upstairs when she heard Sean talking on the phone. She opened the door quietly and listened.

"It's too bloody dangerous. Listen to me: It can't go any further. Keep her out of it." A long pause followed. "If you are sure he wants to stretch it, but nothing.... Oh, you saw her? So you now know the amount of heat I am sitting on." Another long pause followed. "Okay, okay.... Monday." He left the house in a hurry clutching a bag.

Amanda took the phone and pressed last-number redial. It rang for a long time. As she was giving up, somebody picked it up. She recognized the oriental accent of Lynn Li. She replaced the receiver and fetched the Kelly's phone bills. She checked the numbers from Jackie's abandoned bills. Sean and Jackie had been in constant contact since Chrys disappeared.

32

Amanda was back in Southampton to see Doreen. She had finished her exams and wanted to drink. Amanda took her to The Gate, a pub on Burgess Road.

"Are you still pretty close with Sean?"

"Sure."

"What is Jackie's business in your relationship?"

"Search me, love."

Amanda gave up and paid for their drinks. Doreen was as sloshed as she could be and wanted to sit outside and soak in some air.

As they walked towards the University, Doreen felt like talking. Amanda listened. At the party, she had a glass or two too many. Somebody took advantage of her sorry state. Afraid Sean would dump her, she didn't cry rape. Jackie, she now believed, knew who it was but would not say. After that, her relationship with Sean nosedived.

"Every little decision had to be referred to Jackie. It was Jackie O this, Jackie O that," Doreen continued. "If they have such high regards for each other, why pitch me in the middle? He says he loves me; she says she has no interest in him."

"It's true; Jackie has her eyes elsewhere. Where was this party held?"

"It is a basement council flat in Tooting area. Some friend of Jackie stays there. Dayo something... Savage. He is an ex of Jackie O at the Lagos Uni where she took her friggin' history degree. He calls her Jay; every sentence starts and ends with 'Jay'."

Amanda knew she was cracking the case when she listened to a message on her Ansaphone asking her to collect ten thousand pounds and wait for further instructions. She called the prevalent 081 number from Jackie's Granby Grove phone bill that was not the Kelly's. A coarse male voice with a recognizable Anglophone African accent answered. She dropped. The voice got harsher and easily irritable as Amanda rang, dropped, and rang again. She needed to make the person malleable and susceptible to her scheme.

"Hello?" Amanda said, trying very hard to imitate Jackie's flighty voice.

"Jay, *wetin* now?" he said as if he had been waiting for her call.

Click!

At about six in the evening, she called the number again.

"Allo!" a shaky, female voice answered.

"Is Jackie there?" Amanda requested.

"Seen 'er come an' go with Dayo bleeding Savage!"

A very helpful girl, Amanda thought as she listened. "He an' that fancy, foul-mouthed bitch he say is 'im cousin...."

"Oh, my God!" Amanda exclaimed, faking friendship.

"Somethin' of yours them borrow? Won't surprise me; them two are...." she stopped suddenly. "You related to them?"

"Oh no," Amanda added quickly.

"You was lucky! Lis'en, am Beryl. You wan' to come over 'ere and check, you're welcome." She gave Amanda the address. "An uncle is 'ere waiting for them. Seen him in the basement flat before. If am not 'ere, the key is under them flower pots... the one with no flower in it."

"Thank you very much, Beryl."

Amanda couldn't stop wishing there was a little Beryl in everybody. As long as she was not made the governor of the Bank of England, all would be well with the world. She called Pete at home and got his mother. They had met before and, luckily, Lady Anne remembered. She gave Amanda Pete's mobile phone number.

Within the hour, Pete arrived with Sean. She was giving them the address when the phone rang. She picked it up, removed her earring, and said: "Yes?"

"Listen carefully, woman: If you want to see your husband alive, send Sean Kelly with the money to Terminal Three, Heathrow Airport. NOW! You have only two hours; no more, no less. No jokes, be there. If you call police, he's dead dog meat!"

"Go to hell, you slimy scumbag!" She dropped the phone and turned to Pete. "Please proceed to this address. Smash the door, if the pot has no key." She was visibly shaken. She borrowed a cigarette from Sean to calm her nerves, her first puff since she came back to England.

"What are we supposed to be looking for?" Pete asked, picking his words carefully.

"Chrys! Avoid the police like a plague. Any stupid talk and you will all be in for 'Project Promotion,' 'Project Perry,' 'Project Prisoner,' and 'Project Paperback.' Next question?" Amanda smiled a little to the surprise of both Pete and Sean.

"And, if I may ask, what is this operation called?" Pete was trying to be funny.

"Project Pennylove, Pee!" Amanda declared. "Like 'Project Pukemark' that started it all, I want you to handle it."

Pete and Sean walked into the house. Chrys was sitting in the lounge. His eyes were glazed and in need of sunlight, but he looked well. Beryl was in the kitchen cooking something and making a lot of fuss about "them two prats."

"Hello cowboys," Chrys said. "Still sailing the high seas?"

"You didn't lose your sense of humour! Let's get out of here, please," Pete said. "Amanda will roll over us if we delay."

"Is she all right?"

"Yes. What cobblers has MD of DOS International been feeding you?"

Amanda was waiting. They hugged and laughed. Chrys was dying to tell her how much he had missed her. She told him all about the babies. He lifted her off the ground and swung her around.

"Chiké!" Amanda cautioned.

"I think I ought to shove on," Pete announced.

"Me too, Mandy," Sean said smiling.

"Thanks you guys. Remember: mum is the word."

"My lips are zipped," Sean said and made a sign of the cross on his lips.

"Hey, whatever works," Pete concurred.

Amanda took charge of informing the police and arranging a medical check-up. There was no need for debriefing or psychotherapy. She was not telling what happened. She didn't know then; or, rather, she wasn't sure yet.

Chrys's casualness to his ordeal was of concern to Amanda. There was still much more than she had uncovered, a missing link, something that made the incompleteness of the puzzle obvious. She decided to dig a little bit deeper.

33

The news was tucked away in filler columns of a few newspapers. Obviously, they had milked the story dry. Three days later, Chrys gave a simple statement to Southampton Portswood police. The case was straightened out: It was a kidnap-and-extortion racket by a Nigerian gang. The Nigerian police would be contacted through the Interpol to update their records and to keep looking for the chief scammer who was on the run, as evidenced by the recorded ransom demand.

Amanda was waiting in the car and soaking the sun in front of St. Denys Road police station. Chrys opened the driver's side, entered, and heaved a sigh of relief.

"All right?" she asked.

"Belt up, please." Amanda crossed and hooked up the seatbelt as Chrys reversed and drove out of the station.

Two days later, they had settled Ivy's bills, picked up his thesis, and fixed a date for the viva.

Back in London, Chrys was on the balcony overlooking the park in Kensington, his head held in his hands. Amanda had hinted that she might have sown the seed of the scam in Sean's head by suggesting jocosely that only a publishing scandal would make him money. She might have sown the idea, but it was not her fault; he was being unreasonably angry, and he knew it. Solemnly, he mumbled Reinhold Niebuhr's Serenity Prayer: "God grant me the serenity to accept the things I cannot change, the courage to change the things I can, and the wisdom to know the difference."

Amanda came out, handed him a glass of water, and went back to the room without saying a word. He drank it and looked up to admire courting house swallows. He had seen the pair extracting radiator-trapped insects from under the bonnet of a high-performance car parked in front of the house. Chrys wondered whether swallows quarrelled and whether the source of man's problems was his ability to talk, read, write, and own things. He wondered in vain: There are just too many things in life that human beings do not understand, will never understand, and cannot change, even if they have the shine and serenity of Sirius, the stamina and strength of Samson, and the shrewdness and savvy of Solomon.

He went into the living room and crashed onto the couch. Amanda approached and sat besides him. Slowly, she put her right arm round his shoulder. He startled a little. She massaged the back of his right ear and whispered incomprehensible but sweet something into his left ear.

"It's all right," he acknowledged, turned, and looked at her. He kissed her.

"I am sorry," she said, rocking his frame. "You know what you always say about being sorry?"

"Yes, I remember: Sorry soothes the soul."

Luckily for husband and wife, the gas was on low; otherwise, the house would have turned into Mount Etna by the time they returned from Mount Eros.

Amanda first smelled burning food and rushed off to the adjacent kitchenette with a wrapper around her amplified postnatal bosom, her hair dishevelled, and the outline of her gorgeous but fleshier body showing. "Auntie Mary, help us!" she screamed.

Chrys was putting on a pair of boxer shorts in readiness to rush to her help when the phone rang. "Are you okay, darling?"

"I can manage. Get the bloody phone," she said from the smoky kitchen.

"Hello?" the caller hollered.

"Any new scam schemes, Agent Double-O-Cross?"

168

"Isn't Mandy there?"

"She is...." Chrys listened and heard Amanda chucking scraped-out content of the pot into the bin. "She is attending to the soot that was supposed to be Chicken Marengo, our lunch. We will phone for a pizza feast or stir-fry something."

"I hope we didn't overdo it," Sean continued with the tone of an accomplished conspirator.

"What are you talking about, young man?"

"Come on, Chrys; calm down."

"I'm calm, as calm as chilled Chilli Concarne can be."

"Okay, have you squared with Wonder Woman?"

"Sean, call me when you are sober." He replaced the receiver.

"Who's that?" Amanda asked as she walked into the room chewing a large carrot with rather noisy abandon. He offered Chrys raspberry fool, the dessert.

"Sean Kon-elly! Who in the world is 'Wonder Woman'?"

"Jackie O," Amanda responded, grinning widely.

Amanda called Sean later. "How much are you talking about?"

"Four bloody monkeys."

"Some monkey business," Amanda said and then realized what Sean was saying. "Two thousand quid? You must be out of your frosty mind."

"Mandy, you don't believe me?"

"Of course, I don't."

"What was that all about?" Chrys asked as she sat beside him. "What is Jackie's place in the matter?"

Amanda explained, "I think she was the coordinator of Project Prisoner."

"You knew all along that it was Jackie?"

"I suspected."

"I'll kill her!"

169

"She is in Lagos."

"Even if she is in Siberia or in Liberia, I'll find her and she's dead. I'll make sure Sean Simpleton and Jackie Jackass pay for their lies."

"Forget Jackie; go get pizza before we breed ulcers." She decided not to tell him about Jackie and Doreen and what was in it for Jackie. She still speculated his frame of mind.

The next day, Chrys and Amanda were summoned to the Kellys. Sue was there. Sean had sung, and Seamus wanted it in stereo.

"Chrys, I am disappointed in you, both of you... all of you. And you, Mandy, what were you thinking? Here, have a look!" Seamus gave Chrys a copy of his Southampton police statement, which Arinze had faxed from Enugu. "This paper is a tissue of lies!"

Chrys looked at Amanda. She shrugged.

"Okay, Amanda Arinze, let's hear it," Sue sternly demanded.

"Mom, Chrys has absolutely nothing to do with it. The statement was to keep the police off our back. We thought there was no point in stretching the ordeal. It was all Sean's fault." She went on to tell it as she saw it.

"Sean Kelly, is that true?" Sue demanded.

"Jackie O came up with the idea. Chrys complied, thinking that Amanda and the kids were in danger. Jackie O and Dayo took it from there. I was kept in the dark thereafter. I played along believing that Chrys was in it and that he didn't want Mandy to know." Sean stopped, stood stiff, and then looked around. There was no reprieve. His eyes settled on the jumbo-screen television, but he could still hear himself breathe. He felt the taunting of ten tormenting eyes. "Look!" he screamed suddenly as though something stung him.

"What?" Seamus said, surprised by his son's sudden behaviour.

"The author!" he began, pointing at the muted television, his voice vacillating. "THAT!"

'That' was a BBC 2 program: *The Late Show*. Salman Rushdie was talking to Toni Morrison about her latest book, *Jazz*. Amanda and Chrys looked at each other. They got the message. The others looked lost.

"What?" Amanda asked of Sean knowingly.

"You...." Sean's tongue was coming unstuck. "You said 'Do a Rushdie and you're in loads of money.' 'Repeat Rushdie,' remember?"

Amanda was expecting it. "Damn you, Sean, it was a joke in a long long-distant telephone conversation. You know it! Besides, I didn't tell Jackie O, did I?"

The eyes went back to Sean: "No, but Jackie O was here with Doreen while we spoke."

"So?" Chrys intervened, putting his hands round Amanda as if to protect her from an unseen danger. "You were not on speakerphone, were you?"

"No, but I shared the joke, didn't I!" Sean sounded as if he should therefore be exonerated.

Amanda was furious. "Dimwit, I'll tell you what else was shared: Doreen didn't tell you about her pregnancy because she thought it was for some creep, whom she was too drunk to resist or recognize. You didn't admit violating her because you heard what she said she would do. How? 'THAT,' my dear, is the key: Jackie knew. With me out of the way and for some ancient reasons, she weaselled her way back to Chrys. She linked you up with Dayo Savage. For being so beastly to Doreen, she blackmailed you to make Chrys pay for dumping her, not just for any other woman but for me. Your varied and selfish agenda made it easy for her. Even Pete, who has been washing his hands like Pontius Pilate, orchestrated the ordeal knowingly but with enough rope to bail out if it exploded. Of course, Chrys didn't know any better, which was what saved the situation. He thought staying away would save us all further aggravations."

Amanda paused and looked at Aunt Pat. She was visibly shaken, like a mother hen that had hatched two viper eggs. "What have you two done to us?" she whimpered.

"I'm so sorry, Auntie," Amanda said and looked it. "I was trying to save you and everybody else earthly embarrassment. We wouldn't have lied to the police otherwise."

"The whole shebang is simply a stupid, scandalous scam," Seamus stated.

"Who the heck is this eerie angel from hell called Jackie O?" Sue was visibly perplexed.

"She is the only child of Obiageli Nebo, Dad's girlfriend at Oxford."

Bar Amanda, everybody was gobsmacked.

POSTSCRIPT
The bight of blight

Doreen called on Amanda, as she had been doing since she moved back to London.

"Where is Chrys?" she asked as Amanda fetched drinks. "I was hoping to tease him."

"Tease him about what?"

"You wouldn't want to know," Doreen said light-heartedly.

"Try anything silly and I will lace your drink with acid," Amanda teased as she approached.

"It's Jackie's birthday today. In 1990, he said nothing would keep them apart on this day, even if they didn't marry."

"Well, he didn't know there was a girl called Amanda. Anyway, Jackie is not in the country."

"Says who? The Lagos Law School doesn't open until October, or so she said. Sean saw her yesterday on Oxford Street."

She dropped Doreen's drink and went for the telephone with hers. "Ossie, it's me. Amanda."

"Beauty-full Amanda: the wife with whom my soul sails seven seas and my mind moves many mountains!"

"Ossie, may I speak with Chiké, please."

"Chiké?"

"Yes, Dr. Chrys Chiké Chimé—your cousin, the man with whom you were supposed to be meeting—my husband."

"Oh, the meeting is not until later this evening. Listen, as soon as he arrives, we'll call you, okay?" He dropped without asking her what was wrong.

"Don't you think you're being a bit paranoid?" Doreen wondered.

"No, Dor," Amanda said, shaking her head and looking like a sack of flour relieved of its content. "I have a gut feeling that somebody fed me porkpies."

"Do you want me to leave? I wouldn't mind."

"No, no, it's okay," Amanda assured her.

There was a lot to talk about: Fergie photogate, Diana phonegate, and Camillagate. Doreen knew when to stop talking to herself. The motor-mouth had just done it again: Telling Jackie about seeing Chrys and Adaora had split them.

Amanda went to work as soon as she closed the door behind Doreen. She had been doing some mental workout while Doreen went on about Jerry Hall and Mick Jagger, Mandy Smith and Bill Wyman, John McEnroe and Tatum O'Neal, etc. As far as Amanda was concerned, these celebrities did not deserve a second of her time.

It took deft telephone-detective work to discover that Jackie was in town and that she was celebrating. Someone had overheard her suggesting Suya Joint, around Elephant and Castle.

She picked up the phone to call a cab. Behold, the car key was behind the bottle of Jamaican Malibu she had used to prepare Doreen's Bailey Boo.

When she walked into the busy Joint, the background noise ebbed. Chrys and Jackie were the last to notice: They had eyes only for each other. Jackie lowered her face in readiness to take the first blow.

"Happy birthday," Amanda said instead.

Jackie raised her face and saw the "you-trollop" smile Amanda wore. "Thank you," she said, surprised, relieved, but still apprehensive.

"Smashing," Amanda responded. As Chrys began to speak, she gave him a stiff stare. He backed down. She turned to Jackie: "As you grow up, you will find out that our estimable elders have figured out the fundamental philosophy of life." She dragged a chair and sat on it, the backrest in front. "You see, a lamb that would grow horns should first reinforce its neck. If it succeeds, it must not go out with wolves. Why? It will be eaten after a fruitless night-out. Chew on that, my dear Jacqueline."

"Pipe low, Mandy," Jackie said, trying to bolster her confidence.

"You are not talking to me, or are you?" Nobody spoke, not even Chrys. "Smashing. Now, honey, move it." He looked up apprehensively. "I want a quiet word with her."

"Excuse me, Jackie," Chrys said, drained his drink, stood up, and left.

Amanda had nothing more to say to Jackie. As she made to leave, Jackie suddenly stood up. Both hands on her waist, she snarled, "Just a minute, Amanda: who the hell do you think you are? Queen of the world? What gave you the flaming audacity to foul my day?"

Amanda walked back. "Kill me with love! I caught you with my husband and you worry about your bleeding day?"

"*Caught*?"

"Don't shout, you flaky fool," Amanda hushed. "Sit down."

"You think you are smart, don't you?" Jackie continued, sitting down and lowering her voice anyway. "You wouldn't have *my husband* a minute longer if I tell him about your college life. You cannot reap where you didn't sow. Anyway, blood does not lie."

It was infantile to broach the subject of her alleged *supé* affair or her premarital pregnancy; none was a matter of the moment. It was insensitive to allude that Sue snatched Arinze from her mother on her birthday three decades before. The two situations were different.

175

Above all, the blood of Arinze ancestry flowed in their veins. Amanda brought it home to her. It dawned on Jackie that she was wrong. She had just wanted to throw something at Amanda.

Subdued, she soberly said, "Sorry."

"So you should be," Amanda retorted with a reassuring smile. She patted Jackie lightly on the back of her outstretched manicured fingers. "Listen, men are mostly immature, and they have no undying love for womenfolk. Let's stop behaving like bitches, fooling around this dog like he is a god. You are better off without Chiké Chimé, my husband, just as your mother is without Emeka Arinze, my father. Look at my Mom: all alone out here, an oasis of poverty in a desert of wealth. Compare with your mother: a dean of law and married to a Supreme Court judge."

Chrys would have stood his ground in another setting, but his house was on fire; he couldn't afford the ridiculous folly of hunting rats. He knew he was beaten. He wished Amanda had slapped Jackie, poured wine on him and or on her, anything but the seemingly civilized approach.

"I don't want to go home," he said as they crossed the Thames on Westminster Bridge. The left-turn lights by the Houses of Parliament turned from amber to red. She stopped and looked at him askance. "Let's go to Plaistow," he requested.

Amanda laughed. "Oh no, this is between us—you and me, unless you want to admit that you couldn't pull off a clandestine rendezvous with Jackie O." She went round the Parliament Square and turned left into Great George Street. She sped down Birdcage Walk towards Buckingham Palace to avoid the tourist-infested Westminster Abbey and Victoria. "Why are you so uptight? If you are worried about Jackie, don't. She's not a fool. Any girl who plays the field knows the missus might find out and fight back. Instead, let's go back to the house. I will change into something sober, and we will walk to any pub and talk." She took his silence as approval.

They walked across the Holland Park, between King George VI Memorial Youth Hostel and Cricket Field. They walked on in silence past Commonwealth Institute. The pub on Kensington High Street was quiet for that time of the evening. Chrys got a pint of beer for himself and vodka and lemonade with loads of ice for Amanda. He sat down and lit a cigarette.

"Mind if I give you cancer?" Amanda said jocosely.

"Excuse me?"

"Relax, man. I feel like enjoying myself with my husband, getting drunk, and getting laid. Oh, you can pretend I am Jackie for tonight, just for tonight."

"I thought we weren't going to talk about her."

"Make me." She gave him her empty glass. "Straight double, darling… no ice." Chrys looked at her, disbelief in his eyes. "Don't be stingy; you didn't take her out on pennies."

She was into her second straight-double within an hour of feeding Chrys the supermarket-checkout tabloid junks Doreen had fed her.

Chrys had no interest in who was divorcing whom. "You don't think I have anything to do with Sean's scam?" he asked pointedly.

"Oh no! The scam was an ingenious copycat, according to Uncle Gerry, but you played your part, albeit not pre-planned. Staying out of circulation to take the heat off the book was considerate. That you thought of my safety was cool too. What I still don't understand is the lies."

"Lies, what lies?"

"What lies? You are a compulsive womaniser and a pathological liar. Of course, all womanisers are liars, even if not all liars are womanisers. For starters, you were swinging Jackie all through your so-called 'kidnap ordeal.' You wanted me to believe you would want to see her shot. Don't interrupt me, please."

He sat back, hurting and aching.

She continued, "If it were not for the family, I would have the DPP throw the University of London Law Library at Pee Alott. In this age of cyberspace, it would take a few computer key strokes to unravel the racket. You see, you guys left many loose ends. One, Jackie came for certain things you needed; Ivy saw her. She left something behind, but more on that later.

"Two, there is a basement flat below Beryl's, venue of the infamous party. Dayo stayed there before he moved in with her. You paid the rent, but Dayo wanted extra cash. So he shoved Sean off the scam and raised the stakes. He was one more hand in the soup too many. Bad move.

"Three, Pee paid out a thousand pounds to Jackie. She bought the Apple Mac Plus, and you wired it to the Internet. You compiled the references to your thesis. Jackie soft-bound and submitted it. Then you wrote *The Sandhurst Connection*. You proofread her final-year project around Easter vacation. I saw the copy where you queried some reference numbering. By the way, your emails with *Wonderwoman*, Jackie's email handle, are still out there on the Internet."

"What does the boring Colombo crap prove?"

"Four," Amanda continued, ignoring the interruption, "I was naive. You never really got over her. You locked it inside you and ran away from Southampton. You met me on the rebound. You thought I needed a man, when all I needed was a chunk of challenge. Well, you gave me both. Do you know that you never told me about you and Jackie?"

"I didn't want any complications."

"Ha," she snorted. "That must be the understatement of the decade."

"You didn't tell me she was your junior in high school and a second-cousin and that she knew all about you."

"Well, that's all in the past now. We will leave earlier to start planning for the postponed wedding. We must put a smile on our folk's faces. We will get decent jobs and raise the children together. We will make that girl you always wanted, me and you together … oops, you and I."

"What about *The Sandhurst Connection*?"

"There will not be a second book while the military is in power. From what I have heard, the coming months will be very eventful. I am not going to live in Nigeria wondering which parcel would explode. Pee Alott does not know what he is publishing. He could only access the information you used because of his father's connections. Write novels, if you must write. Leave the world to revolve on its axis and to evolve on its own steam."

"And if I say no, what will you do? Divorce me?"

"Chiké dear, don't fight me; if you fight me, you fight an octopus. Don't fight me; fight me and you will have one hell of fight. Please do not fight me."

"Bulls! You walk, we go our separate ways." He was spoiling for a fight.

She picked up their glasses. He made to get up. "My call," she said, smiled, and walked over leisurely to the bar.

He sat back and lit yet another stick.

"No, I won't do that," Amanda continued as she sat down, their glasses refilled. "No, I will not divorce you because, strictly speaking, I am not married to you. Many people are involved. I cannot take the children without a messy fight, and I am not going to bring them up alone while you set sail into the sunshine with, perish the thought, Jackie. I won't divorce you. Our parents do not deserve the hassles. I can't hurt them because that would be a kick in the teeth for their love and loyalty. No, I am not Gina Giacomelli."

She sipped her drink and continued, "What will I do? I may be wrong, but I think I really love you. This thing called love breeds instant insanity. The novelty has washed, but I'll give the marriage my best. It will take more than seven Jackies to stop me. If anybody can keep you tethered, that person is Adaeze Arinze—me."

"The almighty Amanda!"

She was used to his loose missiles, but this short-range edition raised the stakes. "Now, recall I said Jackie left something of yours at Ivy's?" Chrys nodded. "Your personalized Five-Year Diary. Ossie brought it home last December. I read it because I was looking for clues; otherwise, I wouldn't have. You know, what they say about diaries is true: You keep one, one day it will keep you."

He was getting fed up with the carefully calculated and cold process of putting him down. "What is in there that's criminal?"

"Let me put you out of your misery. Picture this: I tell Dad you had an affair with his wife, my so-called stepmother."

"What?" Chrys choked and coughed out some of his drink. "You will do what?"

"You heard!"

Disbelief was written on his face. He looked lost. "Don't be silly," he managed to say before trying to formulate an explanation. "Amaka *was* my girlfriend; it is common knowledge."

"Oh no, the affair happened as recently as the summer of 1990. She was in London. My sister Mary saw you."

"Come on, it would be strange if we didn't meet."

"Sure, but that *meet* was for four weeks of meat-management, a forerunner to your seven-month hibernation with Jackie. You pretended that you had never been to the house, why?"

"Nothing happened," Chrys lied needlessly.

"Tell that to the touring Tunisian Tuaregs, as Dad would say. No wonder I had to drag you into the house kicking and screaming. The day I left, it was Sharon that kept you a minute longer."

"Me and Sharon?"

Amanda smiled. She was enjoying his discomfort, but she wanted to stay the course of driving fear into him. "No! She thinks the world of you; besides, she is *supé* for real."

"Sharon is a lesbian?" Chrys was visibly surprised, but he had a more pressing problem than Sharon's sexuality. He tried to brush off the allegations. "Anyway, you weren't there."

"I was not there, but you recorded it for posterity."

A man should know when he is beaten. It is like having a housefly perch on a ripe scrotal boil: You can't hit it and you can't let it because, ouch or yuck, none is pleasant.

Chrys realized that whatever charm Jackie possessed had an effective antidote in Amanda, an antidote against *Chrysomania* — a compulsive and uncontrollable desire to revisit the nest of old flames. He had hoped to serve as senior special assistant to Senator Arinze. With Amanda and four children in Enugu, and probably carrying another, he and Jackie would set up nest in Abuja. Whoever said, "Man proposes and God disposes," had it wrong: Man merely mocks about with destiny. Amanda was his destiny.

The bell rang for final orders. They had had enough. Amanda drained her drink and said, "What we have here is the avenue to an understanding, if not a happy, married life. I didn't want to say, let alone use, these facts. However, when you bite me on the butt, despite the danger of sinking your teeth into faecal matter, I will bite you on the head and disregard the danger of sinking my teeth into cerebral matter."

Chrys nodded approvingly at her effective use of the popular Igbo proverb.

"Thank you." She continued, "I had my doubts about you and Jackie, but the thought that you could be with her tonight got my knickers in a twist. Forget about us for now; I've vented, and we will weather this teacup storm. Think about Amaka: the picture-perfect political partner of a potential president of Nigeria. I know my father. He is not your average Joe Doe. She would be out in the street before you could say 'Holy Milingo.' He has done worse things to women for lesser sins. I don't give a toss about his politics nor about his ambitions; so, if you dare me, I will strike. We won't want anything happening to your long-suffering, loyal, and loving senior girl at the port of her triumphant entry into political paradise, would we?"

"No," Chrys conceded.

"Smashing!"

Chrys was completely cowed by what he considered "a classical case of amorous blackmail." In 1990, he had labelled her actions "belated blighted blues," and he was going to apply the term to Jackie's family-feud solitaire. Amanda had now become the bight of blights, aggravating both cyst and crawl and bringing out the worst in everybody. He dreaded what else was in her handbag of hubris, for she could be a captivating silly snob, sometimes cocky and sometimes tacky. So he forced her hands: "What else?"

"Sincerely speaking," she said sweetly, still smiling smugly, self-satisfied, "everything else is embellishment."